ABOUT THE AUTHOR

Born in Atlanta in 1920, Donald
Windham now lives in New York
City and is the author or editor
of twelve books. He is widely
anthologized and has contributed
numerous works of fiction, mem-
oir, and essay to magazines and
exhibition catalogues. He is also a
dramatist and collaborated with
Tennessee Williams on the play *You Touched Me.*
A recipient of a Guggenheim Fellowship in 1960,
Windham was presented the Editor's Choice Award
by the Lambda Literary Foundation in 1997.

Photograph by Sandy Campbell
for the first edition of The Dog Star,
Rome, 1950.

ALSO BY DONALD WINDHAM

NOVELS

> *The Dog Star*
> *The Hero Continues*
> *Two People*
> *Tanaquil*
> *Stone in the Hourglass* (limited edition)

SHORT STORIES

> *The Warm Country*

AUTOBIOGRAPHY

> *Emblems of Conduct*
> *Lost Friendships: A Memoir of Truman Capote,*
> *Tennessee Williams, and Others*
> *1948: Italy* (limited edition)

DRAMA

> *You Touched Me* (with Tennessee Williams)

EDITED BY DONALD WINDHAM

> *E.M. Forster's Letters to Donald Windham* (limited edition)
> *Tennessee Williams' Letters to Donald Windham, 1940–1965*
> *The Roman Spring of Alice Toklas: 44 Letters by Alice Toklas in*
> *a Reminiscence by Donald Windham* (limited edition)

THE DOG STAR

BY DONALD WINDHAM **THE**

DOG STAR

HILL STREET CLASSICS, HILL STREET PRESS, ATHENS, GEORGIA

d

Published in 1998 by
HILL STREET CLASSICS
an imprint of Hill Street Press, LLC
191 East Broad Street
Suite 209
Athens, Georgia 30601-2848
www.hillstreetpress.com

First printing

1 2 3 4 5 6 7 8 9 10

ISBN # 1-892514-09-5

Library of Congress Catalog Card Number 98-87989

Printed in the United States of America by Maple-Vail.

The paper in this book contains a significant amount of post-consumer
recycled fiber.

Cover design by Anne Richmond Boston.

First published in 1950 by Doubleday & Company.

TO FRED MELTON

THE DOG STAR

CHAPTER 1

The dog star rose with the sun and the day was hot as soon as it was light.

In the dormitory of the County Farm School, Blackie Pride, a short blackhaired heavybuilt narroweyed boy of fifteen rose from the bunk where he had lain all night fully awake and clothed in a blue work shirt and a pair of khaki pants held together by a wide glassjeweled belt. His movements were tender and supple. He took a guitar from a nail in the wall beside his bunk and walked the length of the dormitory full of waking boys, down the steps and past the monitors into the sun. The boys all watched but no one spoke or tried to stop him. Up the red dirt road from the dormitory to the highway and along the strip of grass between the highway and the pine trees, he walked looking back over his shoulder until the driver of an open truck stopped and gave him a lift. The driver opened the door of the cab for him to sit inside, but Blackie ran and sat on the rear of the truck, his feet dangling over the highway, his narrow eyes watching the landscape behind him. When the truck started the pine trees on either side revolved slowly backward toward the horizon, the nearer trees pursuing and passing the farther like damned spirits pursuing and overtaking each other; and as the truck gathered speed fields of cotton corn and tobacco sped past. The leaves of the plants were not green but dusky, branches were gnarled and warped, and there were no fruits but withered sticks with poison. Blackie closed his eyes so that he would not see them. Immediately the landscape reappeared on the redblack of his closed eyelids, luminous and negative.

Opening his eyes and reaching for the guitar lying on the load of peaches at his side he tried to play it, but the truck joggled so much that he could not touch his fingers to the strings and he put the guitar down. He wanted to move so badly that he thought of jumping from the truck and running. Only the knowledge that he would get out of the country quicker by remaining where he was restrained him. Restlessly, he looked down between his feet at the highway, spiraling out from beneath the truck like the thread of a screw spiraling out of nowhere, and stared at the recurring black stripes. When he became dizzy he closed his eyes to count to a hundred and see if the outskirts of the city would be there when he opened them. Immediately the highway reappeared in negative, black striped in white, spiraling out of the orangedark. He forgot to count and did not open his eyes again until the sun, which lay like a

8

hot washrag across the back of his neck and shoulders, was removed as the truck bounced over an intersection from the highway to a shaded suburban street, stopped and started in traffic, and finally parked at a curb.

In the Washington Street Produce Market he opened his eyes and jumped free of the truck. The guitar in his hand, he strode past the blue state capitol surrounded by shaded boarding houses and came out into the open sun again by the brown city hall in its yard of peavines. Across one of seven viaducts which cut a path through the metropolis, baring the pavement to the dirty empty sky, he entered the buildingshadowed side streets of the shopping district where cats walked with their tails high in the air revealing their dry buttons and men leaned against the fronts of sandwich stores feeling their back teeth. He did not pause even to wipe the perspiration from himself, and when he entered the old neighborhood which is always left behind next to the business district by the retreating population, he was covered with sweat dripping down the curve of his chest to his stomach and rolling through his eyebrows to his nose. On one side of the wide street into which he turned the old houses remained, obscured by outdoor advertising signs built in their front yards, but on the other side newer cheaper and smaller houses stood in the sun with porches flush to the curb. At the bottom of a hill he turned into one of these, crossed the porch and entered the dark hall, letting the screen door slam closed beside him.

As he stood in the dark hall adjusting his eyes to the sud-

9

den absence of light, Mother's heavy figure appeared, silhouetted against the bright rectangle of the back door, then advanced until she cut off the brightness and enveloped him in a hug and kiss.

Mother held him at arm's length and looked at him with a horsetoothed smile.

—Son, what kind of trouble are you in? she asked.

All the way home he had planned to tell her why he had come, but faced with her coarseness and the heavy odor of her cold cream and perspiration he knew that she would not understand.

—None, he answered sullenly. I just wanted to come home.

—All right, Mother said. Come on back in the kitchen and tell me all about it. I'm too tired to stand up here.

A pot of soup boiled on the stove filling the air in the kitchen with steam like that in a bathroom steamed by a hot tub. Lethargically, Mother gave the soup a stir, crossed the room and collapsed in a chair at the table by the window. Blackie leaned in the doorway, neither in the kitchen nor out of it, and waited to suffer her cross examination.

—Is there a holiday at the school? she asked brightly.

—Naw. I told you I just wanted to come home. And I'm not going back.

—All right. I didn't say you had to go back. If you can get a job I can use a little extra money coming in now. Where'd you get the guitar?

—Somebody gave it to me.

He answered haughtily, shifting the guitar behind him as though he did not want it profaned by her eyes.

—Oooooo, Mother mocked his haughtiness. Can you play it?

—A little.

Standing in the doorway he shifted from foot to foot. Behind his eyes he could feel tears, as though he had looked down from the brightest planet in the sky and was blinded by the still recurring circles of light.

—Who gave it to you?

—A fellow named Whitey Maddox.

He changed the subject and asked about his brother and sisters. Caleb, his little brother, had been adopted by two old ladies across town and though Mother said it pained her very much to let him go, she did not feel that she had the right to deprive him of the opportunity. His little sister, Gladys, was out with some girls somewhere, probably bowling. Pearl was working as a waitress in one of those stands on Ponce de Leon where they sell ice cold watermelon by the slice.

—Since she separated from Bob I've been trying to get her to come here to live and share expenses with me, Mother sighed, but she's still living over in that duplex on Baker Street. Just her and that baby in five rooms. I told her to come live here, but, no, she's got ideas. And it's just as well now that you're home. Besides, that baby makes a hell of a lot of noise crying.

11

In the doorway, Blackie shifted his weight from foot to foot.

—Don't stand there wiggling like that, Mother told him. If you've got to go to the bathroom, go to the bathroom. And get washed while you're there. Lunch'll be ready in a few minutes.

Upstairs in the toilet, he knew that home was the wrong place to have come. He remembered something Whitey Maddox had told him lying across the bunk in the school one day: Home is the place where you don't feel at home. He had not understood Whitey at the time, though he had believed him, but he understood now. Turning up the toilet seat, he remembered telling the boys in the school about the time last winter he had left up the toilet seat and Mother had sat down on the cold porcelain rim. All the way downstairs he had heard her scream as though she were shot. Laughing, he had pictured Mother to the boys at the school, a figure of humor and love, seated reading *True Confessions* and toasting marshmallows over the electric bathroom heater. But now that he was at home with her alone, he felt that Mother was his enemy.

In the front bedroom which had been his before he went away in the spring, he threw his guitar down on the bed and looked around. All of his possessions were gone, his tool chest, his magazines, his clothes, his rocks. Everything in the room was littered with Gladys' dolls and scrapbooks and clothes and cosmetics. In the narrow path which the large furniture left in the room, he crossed to the closet. All the hangers were filled with girls' dresses and underclothes, but up on the shelf, beneath a box of toys and a pile of blankets, he found a pair of his corduroy trousers. He changed from his khaki pants, taking out his glassjeweled belt as he threw the khaki pants on the floor. But the corduroy trousers were tight and he put the belt up on the shelf beneath the blankets where he had found the trousers. Wiping his nose and his eyes on his shirt sleeve, he went back down the hall to the bathroom and washed his face. Beneath the chinaberry tree at the school, on the wide rolling clay earth scattered with fallen berries, he had thought himself homesick. But now he felt as though the place he wanted to be no longer existed in the world.

At the foot of the stairs he met Mother coming up the hall.

—Don't go out, she cautioned him. Dinner'll be ready in a minute.

—I'll be back.

—Where are you going? she demanded.

—Out!

He entered the park by scaling a cliff behind a filling station. The embankment was overgrown with small oaks and was smaller than he remembered. At the far end a red clay bank overhung the green golf course. He looked for a cave in which he had spent the night once early in the spring, but the bank had collapsed and no cave was visible, only red clay. Rushing down the clay, he coasted across the rolling grass on the momentum of his run. In the distance a gasoline lawnmower chugged away trimming a green and the air was full of the odor of warm newly cut grass. At the drive he crossed the pavement to the shade of the trees which circled the lake. Running down the bank to the water he walked around the end of the lake on a path just above the waterline. The lake stank of mud and tadpoles. Dead leaves and empty Coca-Cola bottles lay just below the surface of the shallow water. At the other side he ran up another bank and crossed another drive. Then he crept up the side of a hill beneath the bushes, stooped close over the dry earth littered with chewing gum and candy bar wrappers, ice cream cups and wooden spoons, cigarette and contraceptive packages, bits of torn newspaper, dry leaves, pebbles and broken glass. At the top, he stopped in the shade of a large tree and looked out at the playground.

In the brassy sunlight little children played in a sandbox near him at the side of the drinking fountain, and farther away in the center of the grassless plot a group of boys and girls stood around the metal structure of swings and slides which gleamed silver where the green paint was worn away to the metal. Dusty and Hatchet, their blond faces brownsplattered with freckles and moles, were holding onto the pipe above them and talking to a girl who sat at the bottom of the slide and ignored a boy who wanted to slide down. While Blackie watched, the boy slid down and hit the girl in the back with his feet, and in the commotion which followed Dusty and Hatchet looked up and saw Blackie.

—Hey, look who's here!

—Blackie's back! Blackie's back!

As the group of boys and girls from the swings and slides came to meet him Blackie stopped. He thought he saw a boy from the school among them. He recognized the face of a guy he sometimes sat across from at meals. But when he looked the boy full in the face it was not who he had thought it was and did not even resemble him. He walked on to meet the brothers, but his assurance was disturbed as he acknowledged their greetings.

—When did you get here?

—Just now.

—Is the school closed?

—Naw, I just walked out.

With one arm about each of the brothers' shoulders he walked with them to the swings. The brothers introduced him to the girl sitting on the slide and questioned him about his time in school. For a few minutes he answered all the questions asked him, but when Dusty wanted to know what made him leave the school he replied:

—Too many people here. Let's go down by the lake.

Out of the crowd they walked to the edge of the playground.

—Come and push me, Jo Ann called to Dusty from one of the swings, looking upsidedown at the three boys starting down the hill.

—I'll push you later, he called back laughing and making an obscene gesture with his fingers shielded by his departing figure.

Past a clump of ribbon grass and over the roots of an oak

15

tree they descended the hill. On the other side of the drive at the bottom of the hill a gravel path circled the lake beneath the largeleaved magnolia trees toward the bathhouse and swimming pool. Blackie walked between the brothers, moving the limbs of his heavybuilt body slowly and delicately, sensitized by the grief he was about to put into words for the first time. Monosyllabically, in a gentle voice as though he bore some magnificent weight as he walked between them, he answered the brothers' questions about what he had learned in the school. Then he told them why he had come home.

—My best friend in the school killed himself yesterday.

—Gee, why?

—Nobody knows, Blackie said softly.

All night he had asked himself that question and he had arrived at this answer, no answer at all. Whitey seemed, as far as Blackie could see, to have killed himself for no reason. His suicide seemed a mere gesture, a trick of fate, an accident as though Whitey had not known that holding a loaded pistol to his head and pulling the trigger would result in death.

He said no more, waiting for the brothers to ask the name of his friend, walking between them in reverent silence until Dusty broke the silence asking:

—Know that new girl we introduced you to up at the swing? Her old man killed himself. Her mother works and nobody's home all day but her. She's real hot stuff.

Blackie walked between the brothers, silently, as though

he were listening to their exchange of stories about the girl in the swing. Since he could remember he had spent his summers in the park with the brothers. The three of them had called themselves the little gang, little because they were only three and most gangs had five or six. Mornings and afternoons all summer they had been together, stalking adventure in the park as hunters stalk game in the woods, playing the game of for and against with other gangs, dismissing everyone else as friend or foe, designating as good everything which they did and as bad everything which others did. They had been friends. With willingness, energy, pride and desire they had roamed the park together every day, and at night they had met outside their homes in the after supper dusk, leaning against lamp posts and feeling their forearms, and talked away the night with plans of tomorrow. But now he did not belong with them. He felt toward them as they had always felt toward outsiders, self-sufficient, and yet his feeling was tinged with sadness and doubt. He wondered how he could ever have shared all his thoughts with them. They had been closer to him than his own family, but now they were more distant. He wondered if he could ever have been as self-centered and unfeeling as they were. A sentimental distaste for the past made him see himself with them then as now, pretending friendship but knowing that he was alone, and as he walked between them he pretended that it had always been thus.

As they reached the concrete walk in front of the bathhouse they met Crip. Crip's older brother was a bootlegger and Crip sometimes sold liquor in the park at night. He walked on crutches, his legs shriveled up and his shoulders hugely overdeveloped. Blackie had always disliked Crip because he was deformed, but now he greeted him intimately to show that he was distant to the brothers, and Crip, flattered, produced from beneath his shirt a bottle with a little bit of whiskey in the bottom and suggested that they have a drink to celebrate Blackie's return.

Dusty went inside and bought a bottle of grape soda while they waited for him at the door. When he returned they ducked beneath the shrubs which grew along the granite wall of the bathhouse, and though the grass between the cement and the shrubs showed no signs of a path, beneath the shrubs well worn paths ran in all directions.

It was noon. In the distance a whistle blew. Beneath the midday shadow of the bushes the air was sickeningly hot, like the air in a tent beneath the sun, and reeked of sunbaked chlorophyll and chlorine from the pool. At a ventilator in the granite wall Crip stopped, uncorked the nearly empty bottle and handed it to Blackie. The odor of raw alcohol grated on Blackie's nostrils as he accepted the bottle of whiskey and the bottle of soda which Dusty handed to him and, turning the two bottles up to his mouth in rapid succession, drank. Then he handed the bottles back to Crip, sucked in the sides of his mouth so he would not taste the nauseous alcohol, and turned to the wall so the others could not see the face he made.

On the ground next to the wall an empty drink crate

lay on its side. Setting it on end, he stood upon it and looked through the ventilator into the girls' dressing room.

—Beaver! he whispered.

The fanshaped ventilator looked into a corner of the dressing room where a blond girl was pulling on a flowered bathing suit. She stretched the bathing suit over her hips and pulled the straps over her shoulders. Her body was white as it wiggled into the flowered cloth, but her limbs were as pink as the sky at sunset. When the bathing suit was on she walked out of view. Blackie dropped to the ground and gave his place to Hatchet who was pushing for room at the ventilator.

—She's gone now, Blackie said.

—What did she look like?

—Come on. Let's go swimming and get Blackie to show her to us, Hatchet whispered.

At the entrance of the bathhouse Crip left them.

—Do you still have your guitar? Blackie asked.

—Sure, Crip told him.

—Well, why don't you bring it around to the park tonight and we'll play together. I've got a guitar now, a swell one.

Dusty talked to his uncle who kept the keys to the lockers, and he gave them rented bathing suits and lockers without making them pay. Hatchet winked at Blackie and Blackie smiled. But he was annoyed with the brothers when they were in the locker room. The brothers pretended that the drink had made them drunk. They fell over themselves and

pushed each other off the bench onto the floor as they undressed. Blackie was naked while they were still unlacing
their shoes. He thought them silly and undignified. Scratching himself, he pulled on the wool bathing suit and ran
along the wooden slats toward the shower.

—Last one in is a drunkard.

Again, in the shower, he thought that he saw someone out
of the corner of his eye whom he recognized as a boy at the
school. It was no one he knew when he turned and looked
him fully in the face. But as Blackie walked out of the bathhouse and down the steps into the warm water of the children's pool, compelled to enter it by a wire guard on the
sides of the steps from the bathhouse, he felt strangely as
though for a second he had been in the school, the last
two days had not happened, and Whitey was still alive. He
climbed out of the warm water as quickly as he could and
onto the walk surrounding the pool. The cement burned
the soles of his feet and he ran to the wooden boardwalk
which separated the pool from the lake. Splashing water
onto screaming girls, he ran along the boardwalk to the
middle and dived.

The lake was silent and dark green under water, noisy
and yellow on the surface. Several yards out he came up to
the surface and swam toward the far raft. The water in the
creek behind the school had been clear blue and black,
shaded by cool trees in the midst of hot fields. His body
filled with the memory as his arms shot out before him
spraying water in the sunshine and he wanted to be alone

again. He did not stop swimming until he reached the far raft which was almost at the other edge of the lake and, pulling himself out of the water onto the raft, lay face down on the boards, panting. He stared through the cracks between the boards into the yellowgreen rays of sunshine reflected into the opaque water beneath the raft, trying to divine something which he seemed to associate with sunlight shafted through water. But his mind was blank. His loneliness was in his body. Turning over he shook out the water which had collected in the dark hair over his forehead and looked up at the sky.

—Hey, watch what you're doing, a petulant voice warned.

A handful of water scooped from the lake struck him. He was still wet and did not mind. He laughed and propped himself up on his elbows. The same flowered bathing suit which he had seen through the ventilator was lying stretched out before him, and the girl was looking at him and frowning.

—Every time as soon as I get dry some squirt comes and splashes water on me.

She rubbed her hands along her dry skin, wiping off the drops of water Blackie had shaken on her, and lay face down on the raft again, her head on her arm.

—My name's Blackie, he told her.

Up the back of her figure from her feet to her head, he ran his eyes along her sunburned body, and from her head he looked along his own brown legs. The sun was so fierce that he was almost dry already. His legs were browner than

21

the girl's and longer than he remembered them being before. Hair had grown in spots on his flesh since last summer, on his calves and in the middle of his chest and beneath his arms. The nipples of his breast were rigid, and touching them gently, he said:

—I just got back from reform school.

The girl did not answer, so he flicked a drop of water on her.

—What grade was you in, kindergarten? she asked with annoyance.

—You think you're pretty smart don't you? he asked, his voice still friendly.

—Smart enough, she answered into the crook of her elbow.

—Not smart enough to keep me from having seen you in the dressing room with your clothes off. You had a locker down in the far end.

He intended to make the girl look at him and he succeeded. She raised her head and squinted for a long moment before she lowered her head to her arms and said into the crook of her elbow again:

—Well, you've got my permission to go tell somebody else about it. I want to get some sleep.

He stood up and looked down at her figure, narrow-shouldered and widehipped in the bathing suit, and wondering what he could do to hurt her most, dived into the lake at the very edge of the raft hitting the water flat and splashing it all over the girl.

He swam away with her curses following in his trail. The sun beat on the lake like thunder, and bright orange flakes of sunshine remained glittering before his eyes as he swam with his head down under the water. He swam fast trying to work the discontent out of his muscles, and as he swam a revelation came to him which made him forget the girl entirely. Everyone else had not changed. He had changed. The people were the same as they had always been, but he was different. He was like Whitey whom he had admired and not like the brothers and Mother and the ordinary people with whom he had thought of himself when he was in the school. He was separate for he was the leader of the others. Only the strangeness of the school and the greatness of Whitey had blinded him to this before, and now he saw it so clearly that he became wildly elated.

In the shadow of the diving tower he found the brothers waiting for him. He talked to them a moment at the bottom of the structure, then without warning shouted:

—Follow the leader!

And lifted himself up out of the water, clinging to the side of the diving tower, and climbed the crossplanks of its structure up toward the top. From the tower he ran out onto the end of the springboard and flung himself into space, flapping his arms like the wings of a bird and screaming as he fell toward the water. When he rose to the surface, looking up a moment to see if the brothers were after him, he swam into the shadow of the tower and attacked a group of girls who were talking there. They fled in all directions,

23

screaming, and when the brothers caught up with him he dropped the attack and swam underwater from one side of the tower, through the foundations, to the other. There he unwound the latex cord with which his locker key was twisted around his wrist, released it so it would sink through the opaque water into the mud at the bottom of the lake, and dived down to the bottom after it. Skeptically, the brothers pulled the keys from their wrists and dropped them also, anxiously watching as they wavered and disappeared into the darkness. Hatchet came up without his and had to dive again. Blackie did not wait but climbed the tower and lay in the sun, exhausted, listening to the music that floated over the lake from the radio in the lunch room.

He did not talk when the brothers caught up with him and lay down one on each side of him atop the tower. He remained stretched out on his stomach in silence and listened to them tell their secrets. In the evenings they went sometimes to see a photographer on Baltimore Block. They helped the photographer move boxes of plates and he gave them all the real bottled in bond whiskey they wanted to drink. He stayed drunk every night and left his money lying around so it was easy to pick up a dollar if you wanted to.

—Want to go see him with us? Dusty asked.

—Maybe.

—He'll give you all the whiskey you want to drink, real bottled in bond stuff. And he'll take your picture. He's taken both of ours. He makes a lot of money taking pictures of rich folks and don't have nothing to spend it on.

—Sounds queer to me.

24

—He's O.K., Dusty said. He'll leave you alone and you can always borrow money off him. Want to come with us tonight?

—All right, Blackie said.

Rising on his elbows, Blackie pressed his fingers against his chest and when he lifted his hand his skin was white and then red. He had been in the sun long enough. Descending the ladder, followed by the brothers, he waded through the children's pool to the bathhouse. In the shower he washed longer than the brothers and was still beneath the water while they were wringing out their bathing suits. He pretended to himself that he was not even with them, and that he was somewhere else altogether with some other person. When they left the bathhouse and walked back around the path which circled the fish lake beneath the largeblossomed magnolias, the willows and oaks toward the entrance of the park, he walked between the brothers but he did not put his arm about their shoulders. And when they parted at the entrance he waited until they asked him before he made an appointment to meet them in the park after supper.

He walked home by way of the shopping district near Tenth Street. Two five and ten cent stores stood directly opposite each other, one on each side of Peachtree Street. He entered the first and walked past the cosmetics and jewelry and toys and hardware and kitchen utensils straight to the back of the store where the shirt counter was next to the goldfish. There he asked the girl behind the counter for a black shirt.

—Here you are, she said.

She laid a dark blue shirt on the counter before him.

—I want a black shirt, he repeated.

—That's what I'm showing you, she drawled. You can't tell the difference.

Without replying he turned and retraced his steps out of the store. He did not stop until he had reached the shirt counter in the store across the street. The opposition which he had met made him determined. His jaw was clenched. His mind and muscles could not relax. He kept telling himself that he would get the mourning he wanted even if it killed him. But the girl in the second store showed him a black shirt. He paid for it with all the money he had, a squarefolded dollar bill which he took from the watch pocket of his trousers, and the girl gave him a penny change. With the shirt clutched in the hand which had carried the guitar, he walked out of the back entrance of the store and through house-lined back streets toward home, past pale women returning from grocery stores, bags of food in their embrace, and men returning from work, their coats in their hands, wet circles like dark suns beneath the pits of their arms.

Mother gave him a glass of lemonade when he arrived home and did not fuss at him for having been away all afternoon. Gladys was not home yet, and upstairs in the closet of her bedroom, in a cardboard box full of his and his brother's and sister's discarded toys, he found his old knife and whetting stone and lay across the bed whetting the dull knife across the stone until the blade was very sharp. Whitey had

26

shown him the way to get a sharp edge. He tested the knife on his leg, cutting a smooth path through the dark hairs which had begun to cover his shins. In his suitcase at the school he had another knife with a blade better than this, a leather sheaf to keep it in, and a whetting stone wrapped in newspaper. He hoped that his mother would write to the school and tell them to send his suitcase home so he could stay with her. After all, she was more as she had always been than anyone else in the city. His father had been a hero to him—a fabulous man who traveled selling diamond rings on crooked punchboards—and he remembered his father's exploits as he remembered the fabulous deeds of heroes; but his father was no longer an image which he could call into his mind. Mother alone remained real, and as he whetted the knife back and forth across the stone he recalled indulgently the old images which had comforted him in the school: Mother singing a hymn in the kitchen when Father was drunk until Father came and threw the potatoes she was peeling and the bowl and the water all out the door into the dust of the yard, and Mother, without ever ceasing her hymn, gathering the potatoes from the dust and carrying them back into the kitchen. And after Father had died, killed in a wreck as he started out on his first honest job, Mother at Sunday night supper finishing her afternoon date with her boyfriend, making the children set the table, and standing on a chair to look for her jar of hot sauce on the kitchen shelf, cursing and throwing boxes of grits and cans of tomatoes into the corner of the room until she found it.

Or at night, Mother breaking the kitchen chair over her boy-friend's head because he laughed at her, or knocking Pearl through the door because she talked back to her, and stamping indignantly out of the kitchen as though she were the victim of her own assaults. And he recalled these images with humor, not with depression, for even events which seem depressing are relief when their strength drives a path through the endlessness of time—and behind his memory gaped the realization that he could live to be as old as the brothers, or as old as his sister Pearl, or even as old as Mother, but that he could never see Whitey again.

He put away his knife and went down to the kitchen. Mother was mixing cornbread batter in a bowl. He came up behind her and put his arms about her neck.

—Well, that's more like it, she said.

After supper he went to see Pearl, taking his guitar and his black shirt with him. Pearl lived on the top floor of a duplex on Baker Street. He mounted the long outdoor flight of stairs and knocked on the door. The glass rattled emptily through the house. She was not at home. He could see through the glass into the hallway and the rooms off the hall all the way to the back and out through a window to the pale sky behind the building. The rooms were dark and empty.

Blackie did not like to be alone. While he walked further from Mother's and toward the park, just as the long summer dusk was beginning, he thought of how it had been at this hour in the school when all the boys returned from the

28

fields together and washed up for supper. His heels clicked on the sidewalk as they had clicked then along the floor of the dormitory. In the school, though he had been Whitey's special friend, Whitey had stood apart and spent much of his time alone and Blackie had been friendly with all the boys in the school. Now as he descended a hill between vacant lots overgrown with kudzu vines covering sign boards and trees and fields in one flowing greenblack shape, the memory of the crowd pursued him, and he wished that he were with a crowd.

At the bottom of the hill the orange neon sign of the Cuban Villa flashed on. He had always heard of the Cuban Villa as a café run by bootleggers, but he had never been inside. Now he remembered that Crip's brother ran the Cuban Villa and he wondered if he might not find Crip there. A picture of himself in his black shirt sitting around a table of bootleggers, older images of the boys in the school, and answering their questions about his mourning, rose before his eyes. He cut across the gravel yard from the sidewalk to the building. The Cuban Villa originally had been a fruit drink stand in the shape of an orange. Two square additions had been built, one on either side of the oval, and the building was illuminated by an orange sign in front announcing its name and dyeing the air above the building a dirty purple. Blackie pushed open the screen door and entered the room full of amber lights. People were seated drinking beer in the booths on either side of the round concrete ball, but no one was behind the counter in the center

29

of the café. He swaggered up to the counter to show that he was not afraid and laid his guitar down. When he looked up he saw the face of a big dark man who had appeared through the door in the back wall.

—Is Crip here? Blackie asked.

The man did not answer but asked what he wanted.

—Is Crip's brother here then?

A blond man appeared behind the counter beside the dark man and stared at Blackie with the same cold stare.

—What do you want with him? the dark man asked.

—I was supposed to meet Crip here, Blackie said.

—Yeah? Well, I'm his brother and he don't ever come here, the dark man told him.

—Can I buy a drink? Blackie asked.

—We don't have no soda on ice, Crip's brother told him.

Blackie had meant whiskey, but he remembered that he had spent his dollar bill for the shirt.

—He's under age anyway, the blond man said. How old are you, kid?

Blackie tried to think how old he should be to be of age, sixteen, eighteen or twenty-one. Frightened, he dropped his eyes to the guitar on the counter, then, afraid that his eyes looked frightened, raised them again to the faces of the men behind the counter and stared silently. He knew that most of being tough is in acting tough and getting a reputation for toughness. No one had dared fight Whitey, who had been really tough, just because they thought that he was. So he stared at the men, believing that if he turned and left they

30

would never respect him and never know that he had just returned from a reform school that morning and that he wanted to be their friend. He thought it would be better for him to fight them and make them throw him out than to turn and leave as though he were afraid and did not belong with them any more than he belonged at home or with those kids in the park.

—Do you know the kid?

The blond man was speaking over his head to someone behind him.

—Sure, a woman's voice answered. He's old enough to have a beer.

—All right if he's with you, the blond man answered.

Blackie turned and saw the girl on whom he had splashed water in the swimming pool. He wanted to hurt her in some way, to hit her or shout an obscene name at her. She smiled at him and walked back across the café to a booth on the side. He followed her. She slid in on the bench facing the door and he slid in on the other side, facing her, and put his guitar down on the bench beside him.

—O.K., Mabel?

The blond man had followed them to the booth bringing two bottles of beer.

—O.K., Mabel said and paid the man with coins from her purse on the beer ringed and peanut scattered tabletop.

Then she took a cigarette from a package which lay on the table and lit it. As she inhaled she looked across at Blackie and smiled again. He returned her gaze without lowering his eyes but without smiling. Mabel pushed the cigarette package across the table toward him and raised her eyebrow to inquire if he wanted one. He accepted because he thought she did not believe he smoked.

—Really, you are pretty young to be in this place, she said.

Holding a match to the end of his cigarette, he frowned at her and puffed.

—I'm old enough.

—Old enough for what?

—For anything.

He suspected that she did not believe that he would drink either, so he lifted his bottle and took a long swig of the bitter liquid. Mabel smiled at him and nodded toward the guitar.

—Can you play that thing?

—Maybe.

—You can either play it or you can't, she answered. There's a girl down the hall from me who's got a record of *I Can't Give You Anything but Love, Baby*. Can you play that?

He leaned over the guitar, lowering his head close to the instrument in his lap, and began to strum the strings. He picked notes high and separate, playing very seriously, and did not look up until he had finished the song and put the guitar down.

—Well, you certainly can play that thing. What's it called? she asked loudly.

32

She smiled at him as she spoke and her face made a bright collection of concentric circles about her crooked white teeth like the circles about a stone flung into a pool of water.

—It's a guitar, he told her. A guy in the reform school gave it to me.

—What was his name? Mabel asked.

—Whitey Maddox, Blackie told her.

—That's funny, Blackie and Whitey are the same kind of names. Were you really in a reform school?

—Sure, Blackie said. And I've never known anybody anywhere like Whitey. Even the guys that ran the place looked up to him.

—Yeah, I know the type, teacher's pet.

—The hell he was. He didn't do nothing the teachers told him to. Only they never caught him doing what he did. But if they had of, he would of told them off. He didn't have no use for nobody.

—He sounds like a son-of-a-bitch to me, Mabel said.

—He wasn't no son-of-a-bitch. He was my best friend. I wouldn't say things like that about nobody I didn't know if I was you. I'd be careful.

—I didn't mean anything, Mabel said. Only I don't see what you mean when you say he didn't like nobody and then say he was your best friend.

Blackie thought silently. He was angry and wanted to be sure that he was understood this time. Words did not mean much to him. They were only aids to actions as far as he was concerned. If you did what you said then your words mean

33

what you did. When he had done things which he was told were bad and he had benefited he called the things good, for good always means that which is desired. He did not like having to explain things to a girl he did not know well, but he wanted her to understand.

—It wasn't exactly a reform school, he said slowly. It was a farm school. Whitey used to call it the farmers' academy. But you got sent there by the juvenile court. I worked in a field next to the creek and one day I thought I'd sneak in and cool off. I was working alone and I figured nobody would catch me.

He laughed at the memory of his innocence.

—When I got inside the trees I saw Whitey. His clothes were lying on the far bank and he was in swimming. Everybody was always trying to be his friend, you understand, because he was the toughest guy in the school. But I'd never seen him put himself out for nobody. He didn't even answer sometimes when people spoke to him because he didn't like to talk. I was scared he'd beat hell out of me for catching him in swimming and I was about to run away when he called to me. Come on in, he said. Just like that. Like we were good friends and he was expecting me. I still thought he was going to do something when I got in the water. But he didn't. From that time on we were friends. We'd go in swimming every day and never get caught. And all the time the superintendent was playing up to Whitey because the other boys looked up to him and would do what he said. The way Whitey told me he figured it was that you

34

were dumb if you followed the rules, but that you were dumber if you broke them and got caught doing it. But even after we were friends he still liked to be alone. He didn't like to be touched, ever, and sometimes he'd go off by himself when he knew you were waiting for him and wouldn't say nothing to you about it.

—How'd you get sent to the school? Mabel asked.

Proudly, he told the story to her as he had told it to others.

—Me and a couple of fellows I was in swimming with today got caught staying all night in a cave in the park with a girl. At least, we didn't get caught but the girl's mother found out what happened and told the police we'd done it.

—What could a bunch of little buttermilks like you do? Mabel laughed.

—That's all right, we could do plenty, Blackie told her. But after her mother had got all of us into the juvenile court, do you know what the judge did? He asked everybody what happened and then he said: You boys, go home. And you, young lady, you're going to reform school.

—I thought you were the one that went to reform school, though, Mabel said suspiciously.

—I'm coming to that, Blackie said impatiently. You see, this girl lived next door to me. But we were moving. I had built a club house under our house by nailing some boards around a couple of the brick foundations and I was pulling them off to take with me. They were my boards. I'd gone to all the vacant houses in the neighborhood getting them. But this girl's mother saw me out of her window and called the

35

landlady because of what had happened to her daughter and told the landlady that I was tearing down her house. And the landlady called the police and got me took to juvenile court. And they knew I hadn't been doing nothing wrong, but because it was the second time I'd been there they had my mother agree to send me to the farm school where I'd be off the streets and out of trouble.

—And how'd this Whitey get in if he was so smart? Mabel asked.

Blackie lifted his bottle and drank as he thought about what Whitey had been like and how he had gotten sent to the school by his father whom he hated. But he did not know how to put the story into words to tell a girl, and when he put his empty beer bottle on the table he said:

—You waiting for somebody here?

—I was looking for a girl I know, Mabel told him looking about the room.

—When was she supposed to be here?

—Oh, she wasn't supposed to. I was just looking for her. But I guess she's not coming now. Want to walk me home?

The downtown sky was pink with the reflection of neon. In the July heat the silhouetted buildings loomed like charred coals in a fireplace, their yellow windows last embers. Along the undulating hexagons of cement sidewalk tiles Blackie walked close to Mabel and let his arm touch hers. With someone who had never known him before he realized the intimacy and emotion which he had expected all day. Mabel was almost a woman. She lived in a hotel in an alley

36

off a side street, downtown. At the alley she did not tell him goodnight and he walked her across the lobby and up the stairs to the hall outside her room. When they stopped at her door he put his arms about her shoulders and kissed her. Instead of repulsing him, she kissed him back.

—You're quite a kid, Mabel said. You ought to come see me some night.

—What's wrong with tonight? Blackie asked.

He asked with confidence, but when she gave him the key to open the door he was overcome with excitement. The key was larger than any other he had ever seen, and thinking of her body as he had seen it that afternoon before she pulled up her bathing suit he was so excited that he could hardly put the key in the lock. When they were inside the room, Mabel closed the door and kissed him again without turning on the light.

Later, in the dark, he slipped off the bed and walked to the window. He thought Mabel was asleep, but she was awake and asked where he was going. He did not know exactly what attitude to take to her.

—I want a glass of water.

—There's a basin in the corner and a glass on a shelf above it.

After he had drunk a glass of water he returned to the bed and sat on the edge putting on his shoes.

—I guess I'd better go home, he said.

Mabel did not answer for a minute. Then she asked:

—When'll I see you again?

—Soon.

She kissed him before he went out and as he walked down the hall to the stairs he was conscious of her watching him through the crack of the door.

He was so tired that he did not think about anything. An old man was asleep at the rattletrap desk in the lobby. He slipped slowly past the man and out the door into the alley that led to the street. Through the calm excitement of dark and deserted streets he passed from street lamp to street lamp, crossing their tangent strings of lights diminishing into the dark at each corner. No one passed him. When he reached Baker Street he turned down the hill toward Pearl's duplex for he was afraid to arrive at Mother's so late and have to explain his whereabouts. At Pearl's he mounted the long bare steps to the door and knocked on the glass. Through the door he could see the house just as it had looked earlier, the doors open between rooms and the night sky visible through a rear window. The rattle of the glass echoed through the house, and in the silence which followed he heard his breath and the beat of his heart. Cautiously, a silhouette appeared in the hall from one of the rooms. Pearl came toward the door and peered through the glass at him sleepily. When she recognized him she shook her head as though she had been expecting someone else and called his name. She unlocked the door and threw her arms about his neck. In the hall, whispering so they would not wake the baby, he told her that he had come home to stay. She showed him to a bedroom and whispered goodnight to him

38

from the open doorway as she went back to her room. He put the guitar on a chair, undressed and went to sleep almost at once. Sometime before morning, he dreamed.

He was living in the country in a large house surrounded by a sacred wood. From a long way in the distance a white highway came straight toward the house, and just before the front door swerved off into the woods. Blackie watched a black speck approaching from the distance of the highway until he saw that it was a man walking toward him and that the man was Whitey. He knew that Whitey was dead but he was not surprised. He walked to the edge of the yard to meet Whitey and brought him back into the house. Seeing Whitey made him intensely happy, as though they had been separated a long time. Whitey carried a bunch of wisteria in his hand which Blackie took and put in a vase of sunshiney water. They sat in a room on either side of a table which held the vase of flowers and talked. Whitey looked as though he had been ill a long time and Blackie told himself that was because Whitey was dead. His face was no longer golden but white with green shadows beneath the three mounds of his cheeks and nose; he no longer smelled salty like sweat but sweet like flowers; his summer suit was too big for his body and the collar of his shirt hung loose about his neck. Whitey asked questions about Blackie's family as though it were his own family and Blackie answered. Then Whitey stood up and said that he had to go. Blackie followed him out and wanted to shake his hand, but Whitey said:

—No. You must not touch me.

39

Blackie obeyed and followed him to the edge of the yard where a vine of wisteria hung over the highway shading the concrete. Whitey broke off a branch of the wisteria saying that he had brought purple wisteria and would take back blue. But when Blackie started to follow him up the road, Whitey said that this was as far as he could go; so Blackie stood beside the broken branch of the wisteria vine; and as a green brand that is burning at one end at the other hisses with the wind which is escaping, so from that broken splint, shards, flints and pebbles, the purple bloom of the violet, the scarlet stain of the anemone, the crimson flush of the rose, words and blood came forth together. . . .

CHAPTER 2

The summer's flower was full open, the air outside the kitchen window blazing yellow as the petals around the black heart of a sunflower in the sun. Blackie sat in the open windowsill drinking a glass of milk and watching Pearl dress. She crossed the hall from room to room in her underslip, talking to him as she made up her face and put on her clothing. All the doors between rooms were open. No curtains hung over the large windows where the shades were rolled to the top. Very little furniture obscured the morning light. The apartment seemed to be an extension of the treetops and wires of the backyard and the loading platforms and trucking depots which lined the street in front. Mother had said that the house had no privacy. But Pearl had said that she would rather live in the street than in some of the dark small apartments she had seen and had moved into the duplex with very little furniture, two veneer bedroom suites to spread over three bedrooms and no furniture at all for the diningroom.

41

Pulling down the skirt of her dress Pearl ran into the kitchen and gave Blackie an impulsive kiss.

—Gee, but it's good to have you home, she said. Mother's already called looking for you and raised hell because you didn't come home last night. Some men from the school came by the house asking for you and she claims she had a hard time convincing them you were home. But she says she told them she needed you here and you were out looking for a job. She talked to me like it had killed her to tell a lie, but I told her we'd all come over for supper tomorrow when I don't have to work and have a kind of family reunion and that calmed her down.

—Swell, Blackie said, not wanting to talk about the school or mother: Have you got a cigarette?

—In the bedroom, Pearl answered, evincing no surprise that he smoked. Come on in with me and look at Jeanette. You haven't seen her yet.

He followed her into the bedroom and smiled down at the baby in the crib.

—She'll be a year and a half next month.

Blackie held out one of his fingers and the baby took hold of it, letting her empty bottle slip to the bed beside her and wrapping her five tiny fingers around his one big finger. He was amazed for he had not remembered how small babies were.

—Isn't she smart, Pearl said. Bob's family wanted to take her out to their place in the country and keep her there. I wouldn't have minded too much, but Mother raised such

42

a fuss that I refused to let them and Bob got angry and left. We aren't even speaking now. I guess we didn't get along very well even before that, though.

She went to the dresser and found the cigarettes. Blackie lit two simultaneously, a gesture he had learned in the movies, and gave one to Pearl.

—I have to leave her with the woman downstairs while I go to work. She's got one the same age so it isn't much trouble to her. But maybe it would have been better for her to have been in the country. I know I hate this city. But Mother raised such hell.

She took the baby's empty bottle and carried it back to the kitchen. Blackie sat in the window and watched her while she finished her cup of coffee. Then she left him and went to get her pocketbook. He felt strange and new, but he felt at home in Pearl's house. When she came back into the kitchen carrying her purse and the baby on her arm, she held out a dollar bill to him in her other hand.

—Buy yourself some cigarettes, she said. I've got to go to work now. Good-by.

Blackie stayed in the house all day as though he were recovering from an illness. He sat in the sunlight of the window and looked at the broken alarm clock lying on its side on top of the icebox until he decided to repair the clock. On the dresser in Pearl's room he found some bobby pins and a nail file. He had a tool box, a crate from the

43

grocery store with shelves and compartments made of cigar boxes nailed inside, which would be in the garage behind Mother's house unless she had thrown it away, in which he kept his saw, screwdriver, hammer, and all the locks, hinges, screws, nails, light switches and sockets which he had stolen from vacant houses when he had been leader of the little gang with Dusty and Hatchet. But he did not need more than bobby pins and a nail file to fix a clock.

He took off the round back of the clock. Inside all the parts were circular, spring coils and wheels, and as he took them out he began to think of Mabel. Last night she had told him that he had beautiful hands. He watched his hands as they took the clock apart, and they crossed and picked up and turned as he watched, as though they had a life of their own separate from his will. Each round finger was alive with convex muscles moving slowly and heavily beneath the protruding veins, and though he had always thought of his hands as short and ugly he now saw them as full of power and beauty. He saw what Mabel meant, and as he took out the cogs and springs half his attention was on his work and half on his hands. Calmer than he had been the day before, he released whatever tension remained after the night with Mabel into refitting the parts of the clock. The sun crept over his back and onto his fingers as he finished and he wondered what Mabel was doing and if perhaps she was at this same minute thinking about him and his hands. Then he rescrewed the back on the clock, wound it and shook it, but it would not run. He decided that the clock was no

44

good and went to Pearl's bedroom and took out a broken window weight which he had noticed.

He thought of Whitey as he removed the side from the window and took out the heavy weight. The sun falling through the glass cast a nimbus of light about the shadow of his head on the floor and he remembered the nimbused shadow of Whitey's head on the greenblack water with the sunlight radiating about it in the same way and realized that he was thinking calmly about Whitey for the first time since Whitey's death. He tried to make up his mind what he was going to do. When he left the school he had felt that he carried with him an indebtedness or an inheritance which was his most important possession in the world. He had been too upset at the time to say what it was, but he knew now that he wanted to live as Whitey would have lived. Yet he did not know how that would have been. His conception of Whitey was larger than reality, but it lacked detail. In his eyes Whitey had been able to do no wrong but he was not quite sure what Whitey had done. He had pursued his hero with his senses, as the hunter pursues with dogs to get nearer to the animal nature of the creature he hunts, and he had captured Whitey with his eyes. But he had not abstracted the qualities which made him think Whitey admirable. Now he could not find words to recall those qualities to his satisfaction. The nearest he came were strength and greatness and indifference. Whitey had been strong and great and he had cared about no one. Yet the words seemed thin and abstract for what he had felt he

45

carried with him as he left the school, something as solid and real as the guitar he had carried in his hand. He wanted the words to be as real as Whitey had been standing before him, his face and neck and hair all bleached the same saw-dust yellow glowing with a sheen all colors of the rainbow, each feature separate and calm, but all the same tow color, nose and cheeks three indifferent mounds between mouth and eyes. He wanted the words to bring to his mind the feel-ing of power and happiness Whitey's body had brought to his eyes as it moved in faded dungarees slowly and separately across the fields, and as he recalled Whitey's image he re-peated the words over and over until they absorbed from the image the meaning he wished them to have. Yet did the words expand to the image so much as the image contracted to the words? He could not quite imagine Whitey. He had seen something which is seldom sought and seldom seen by those who seek it—but it was gone now and the fate of the hunter is determined not only by what he seeks but by what he finds.

His imagination could go no further.

Piedmont Avenue was lined with trees. In their shade, shielded from the sun, the lawns were green. Blackie walked toward the park. It was early: he had gone to sleep early and he had awaked early and slipped out of the house while Pearl was still asleep. No children were on the streets at this hour. Cleaner after night than after rain, the pave-ment stretched in deserted quietness except for a few auto-

46

mobiles moving toward town. A garbage truck and a milk wagon passed, and a paper boy went ahead of him throwing newspapers onto porches.

As he walked downhill a few blocks from the park, Blackie saw his little brother, Caleb, leaning against a brick wall in front of an apartment house and looking across the street. Blackie smiled and remembered the last time he and his little brother had been together.

Mother had bought a box of Norris' Exquisite Candy for his birthday in April before he went to the farm school. Caleb had wanted the box top.

—It's beautiful, Caleb said.

—Beautiful, Pearl mocked in her nervous voice. Beautiful, what a sissy word.

Caleb turned away, pretending not to care, wanting the box top. Gladys joined in the taunt.

—Beautiful, what a sissy word.

Caleb turned his back on his sisters and looked at Blackie. They had just eaten ice cream and cake. Blackie was satisfied and ready for some fun.

—Beautiful, what a sissy word.

It made him joyful and secure to join in the fun. Mother, who was examining the pieces of candy to choose one to eat, laughed and told them to leave Caleb alone. But the two girls repeated the words till they sounded with the insistence of a bouncing ball, Blackie laughed, and Caleb, with no one to turn to, looked down at his feet and kicked the ground of the backyard. Blackie slipped up behind him and put his

47

hands on Caleb's shoulders. Caleb turned to see what he wanted, and Blackie whooped in his face.

—Beautiful, what a sissy word.

Caleb swung at him, his eyes blinded by tears of fury, and pummeled Blackie's chest with ineffectual blows. Blackie could hardly feel the fists striking him, but the sight of his little brother's eyes streaming with tears and his mouth twitching with sobs as he shouted that Blackie was evil and would die and go to hell, to hell, to hell, formed a baffled hollow of remorse in him. Surprised, he tried to put his arm around Caleb's shoulders, but Caleb jerked away and continued to hit at him. Mother said for them to give Caleb the box top and to leave him alone. And while Caleb sulked they ate candy.

—Hello, kid, Blackie said.

Caleb was staring across the street and bouncing his buttocks against the brick wall of the apartment behind him. When he heard Blackie's voice and looked into Blackie's face only a foot from him, a smile which he could not restrain opened all the way across his face puckering up his cheeks and jutting forth his jaw. He had not known that Blackie was back from the school (Mother had not called him the day before) and excitedly he asked one question after another. Blackie calmly took out his cigarettes and asked Caleb what he was doing here so early. Caleb explained that he was waiting for a friend of his who was across the street at his aunt's house borrowing five dollars. They had come early in the morning, saying the boy's

48

mother had sent them so his aunt would think the money was important. When the boy came out they were going to take the five dollars and have a good time uptown.

—What's this guy like? Blackie asked.

—He's a friend of mine, but I don't like him.

—Well, then we can have a better time with five dollars without him than we can with him, Blackie said.

Caleb smiled without restraint. In the heliacal stillness of the morning the sun bore down more and more warm as they talked and waited. At last the boy came out of a house up the block and ran across the street toward them. He was a fat-assed kid and Blackie disliked him immediately.

A stream of automobiles was pouring steadily past them toward town now, filling the sunshine with the buzz of tires on pavement and the fumes of gasoline. They left the street and entered the park through a break in the hedge. Dew sparkled on spiderwebs in the grass and surprised birds flew from a tree nearby. With their shoes wet from the grass, they reached the gravel walk which circled the lake and walked around toward the swimming pool. At the far end of the park the mist over the sewerage stream was just beginning to thin, and the air over the lake was foggy. When they reached the boardwalk which separated the lake from the swimming pool, Blackie said:

—What about a boat ride?

Silenced by the joy of shining as a binary star with his brother, Caleb nodded in agreement. The fat-assed boy asked:

49

—Where'll we get a boat?

—We'll take the lifeguard's.

The lifeguard's boat was tied to the end of the boardwalk with a chain through which a lock was fastened. Blackie took a hairpin from his pocket and opened the lock, untied the chain, and told the two kids to get in first. He shoved the boat from the shore and jumped in after them. A brace of ducks padded away from the side of the boat in alarm, but before the boat the lake lay perfectly calm, reflecting the sky, turning from black to green as the sky brightened from blue to gold. Drink bottles glistened in the mud until the water became too deep to see the bottom. Blackie rowed, his two fists revolving rapidly about each other, until they reached the middle of the lake where the water was deepest. Then he told Caleb and the fat-assed boy to look over the side of the boat into the blackness at the bottom of the lake, too deep to reflect light, and while they were looking he imperceptibly shifted the weight of his body and rocked the boat from side to side.

—A man drowned here once and they never found his body, he said.

—Why? Caleb asked.

—Because there's no bottom. I think he probably came up to the surface on the other side of the earth though, in a lake in China.

The fat-assed boy grabbed the sides of the boat with both hands and tried as tensely as he could to hold the boat steady, but Blackie looked farther over the side and water slopped

50

into the bottom of the boat. The fat-assed boy looked straight ahead and exhaled his breath from his lips with a low whistling gasp. Blackie turned toward him suddenly, slapping another wave of water over the side of the boat.

—What's wrong? he asked.

—I want to go back.

—Then pull out that extra oar by you and start rowing.

—I don't know how to row, the kid gasped in terror.

—Well, you'd better learn to row unless you want to stay out here the rest of your life, cause it's all I can do to steady the boat, Blackie told him angrily.

—Why? the kid asked. What's wrong?

—Nothing, just these oars are locked.

The kid tried to turn around and look at Caleb, but the boat rocked and he stopped halfway.

—I want to go back, he said into space. Caleb, make him take us back.

—Hey, sit still, or you'll turn us over and drown us all, Blackie shouted. Just lean back and enjoy yourself while you're here. I'll row you back. But you may as well have a good time, cause it costs you two fifty to be rowed out here and it's going to cost you two fifty to be rowed back.

The kid cried that he did not have any money, but Caleb knew where it was. He grabbed the boy to take the money from him, and the boy was so frightened that he did not resist. He lay back with his face toward the sky and drew in his stomach while Caleb extracted a five dollar bill from the watch pocket of his trousers.

—Is that all he's got? Blackie asked.

—Yeah, Caleb answered. He didn't have no money when we started out.

—You'll go to jail. I'll tell my mother on you and you'll go to jail, the kid sobbed.

—O.K. Go ahead and tell your mother. She'll be glad to know. But cut your sniffling until then or I'll throw you out and let you drown anyway, Blackie threatened.

He lit a cigarette and rowed back to the boardwalk. The fat-assed kid sat in terrified silence until they reached the shore and Blackie tied the boat to the boardwalk. Then he jumped out and ran up the bank. At the top he stood in the bushes looking back at Blackie and Caleb until Blackie suddenly turned toward him and he ran away. Blackie locked the boat and walked up the bank and along the path toward the drive without saying a word. Caleb ran until he caught up with Blackie, and walked along at his heels afraid to speak until he was spoken to. Suddenly Blackie stopped and looked around at him.

—How's that for getting money? he asked.

—O.K., Blackie.

—Then what are you acting hangdog for? Walk up. Have those goodie-goodie old ladies you live with got the best of you?

—I wasn't thinking about them. Honest, I wasn't, Caleb said.

—Then act like a man if you want to come along with me. You're not going to get into any trouble. Take care of yourself and let the world take care of itself. Am I right?

—Sure you're right, Blackie.

—Well, then, come on and stop farting along.

Blackie hitched up his trousers and strode along the gravel path and across the street out of the park. He had wanted to make up to his brother for having been mean to him in the spring and he was annoyed by the implied censure which he had felt in Caleb's hanging back. When people did not say anything, how could you tell if their quietness was dislike or admiration? Maybe he had taken advantage of a kid smaller than he. But the kid wasn't any smaller than Caleb. And the kid had stolen the money, anyway.

On the other side of the street he stopped in a drugstore and bought a package of cigarettes to break the five dollar bill.

—Do you want to split the money and both go our way, or do you want to spend the day with me? he asked Caleb.

—Spend the day with you.

—O.K., Blackie said pocketing the change. Let's go uptown and take in a movie.

They rode uptown on a streetcar. The movie did not open until nine-thirty and they went into another drugstore and ate two ice cream sundaes.

—Do those women you live with give you much money? Blackie asked.

Caleb was sitting beside him with his elbows on the marble counter and spooning ice cream into his mouth.

—No, he answered. They buy me anything I ask for, but they never give me any money.

53

—You ought to ask them for money, Blackie told him.

The house lights were on in the theater and the curtain drawn across the screen. But the theater seemed cool and dim after the heat of the sunlight. Blackie sat with his knees on the back of the empty seat in front of him and waited. Cool and dim in the shelter of the trees, the sand at the edge of the stream had stretched away from the water into the grass and sunlight. Some mornings he and Whitey had lain naked on the sand or in the grass to dry themselves and some they had waded up the narrow mouth of the pool and climbed onto the flat slippery rocks overhanging the sluice where the swift water rushed in. Crawling on hands and knees to a spot where the sunlight fell onto the brown rocks and airwhite water, they had lain down on the unyielding stone their almost equally unyielding bodies, and when they were dry had waded back down the stream, wetting only their feet, and sat in the sand to dry their feet on their shirts before they dressed.

In the theater, flooded with the memory of sunlight sand and water, Blackie turned to his little brother and began to tell him about Whitey. After that day at the creek they had talked at night as they watched for falling stars, Whitey lying in the upper bunk, Blackie in the lower. Moonlight streamed through the many windows of the sleeping porch dormitory so they could see each other; and outside, beyond the chinaberry trees, the night train whistled in the distance nearer and nearer until it crossed the end of the last field, its smoke white in the moonlight, and disappeared, whistling

54

farther and farther until it could no longer be heard. Dogs howled at the moon silver above the barns and fields and trees, and Whitey's words came to Blackie, whispering that he must be tough and strong and indifferent if he wanted to get along in the reform school and even stronger and tougher and more indifferent if he wanted to get along in the world. Whitey told him that he never had felt attachment for his family. He ran away at fourteen with a girl and hitchhiked to California. When they reached California there was nothing there so they turned around and hitchhiked back again. The girl married somebody and had a baby. Alone, Whitey ran away from home and hitchhiked to Florida. In a camp outside Jacksonville, a regular place for hoboes and boys on the road, he lived among grown men and stood up to them. He was as tough as anybody, and when he left he took a guitar which one of the men had taught him to play. He made his way down one coast and up the other performing in tourist camps and roadhouses. At St. Petersburg he robbed an old man of ten dollars and spent all the money on food in one day. When he reached home again he fought with his family and his family sent him to the reform school. He had come because he wanted to see what it was like, and he boasted that he would leave any time he wished. But he seemed happy there. Sometimes Blackie left the other boys and found Whitey alone in the dormitory contentedly playing his guitar, indifferent whether anyone listened or not. He did not need anyone, not even Blackie, his best friend. Then one day he disappeared. He left without saying a word even to Blackie, and Blackie expected never to see him again. But a week later Whitey came back, apparently of his own accord, and was put in the punishment room at the top of the second dormitory. Blackie tried to get in trouble and be sent to the second dormitory so he could see Whitey. But before he succeeded, Whitey shot himself through the head.

When Blackie finished the story Caleb said to him:

—Gee, what do you think Whitey would do if he was with us now?

Blackie did not answer. In the cool dim theater he did not know what Whitey would do or he would be doing it himself. He could only think of Whitey at the school, in the shaded stream or the night dormitory, and when he tried to imagine Whitey in the city the image faded, lost all its details, and only the abstract words he had formulated the morning before remained. Strength and courage and indifference. Then the theater darkened and the movie began.

When he came out into the afternoon sunlight, Blackie was dazed and he wanted to get rid of Caleb. He posed on the sidewalk in front of the theater, self-consciously aware of himself in the sudden sunshine and retaining in his stance and voice the arrogance and independence of the hero who had died in the dark theater but lived on in him.

—Ever go by to see Mother? he asked Caleb.

—Sure, I eat supper with her every Friday.

—O.K. I'll see you there, Blackie told him. I got something to do now.

Alone he walked down Carnegie Way toward Spring Street, melodramatically aware of the world about him, suspended between the bright reality of the afternoon streets and his desire for great actions like those in his dark imagination. He was not pleased with his morning in the park. What he had done was mean and he did not want to be mean. He wanted to find Whitey's place in the city. Yet it was already so hot that as he crossed the street his shoes left their prints in the tar.

Pearl's house was empty. He went to his room and sat on the edge of the bed taking off his shoes. When he was alone he liked to sleep. Sleep blacked out the world of memory and aspiration, and after the dark of sleep the light of new and uncontemplated actions came like the light of day. Alone in the house with no one to talk to he lay across the bed strumming on the guitar to keep his body moving and his mind still. He shut off consciousness as he would switch off an electric light; and images, which later would come out as actions, entered his mind without his ever becoming aware of them, and their muffled meanings blacked out the afternoon and brought on the pleasant dark.

CHAPTER 3

He awoke with sweat rolling down the arch from his back to his buttocks and the sheet wet beneath him. With his eyes closed, he lay and listened to the silence of the late summer afternoon through the window. The silence was an endless ocean and endlessly beyond the ocean stretched a desert of small noises, the echoes of a hammer and the call of automobile horns, the shouts of children's names and the roar of trucks. Across the silence Pearl's footsteps echoed in the hall and the baby gurgled in its crib far, far away. He tried to realize that they were only a short distance from his room and that this afternoon, this day, his whole life would be lived with them, but his mind was gone to sleep as his foot sometimes went to sleep from lack of circulation and he could not wake it. Then he sat on the edge of the bed, pulled on his trousers and walked through the house.

Pearl was in the kitchen heating the baby's bottle and drinking a Coca-Cola.

—Oh, you scared me, she gasped. I didn't know anyone was here.

—I been asleep, he yawned.

—Want a coke? she asked.

—No.

Sandyheaded, he crossed to the sink for a glass of water to wet his tongue which was dry and stuck to the roof of his mouth. When he finished drinking the glass of water he wanted to talk to Pearl but she had taken the baby's bottle from the stove and left the kitchen. Back in the bedroom, as he sat on the edge of the bed lacing his shoes he heard a muffled sobbing across the hall. He called Pearl's name but she did not answer and he crossed to the door of her room and looked in. She was lying prone across her bed with her face in the pillow.

—What's wrong? he asked.

—Nothing.

—There must be something wrong to make you cry.

—I'm tired.

—Is that all?

—Bob came to see me today.

He tightened at the sound of the name as though all day he had been waiting for something to pit himself against.

—Why did you see the bastard? he demanded.

Pearl turned her face from the pillow and looked up at him.

—I wait on tables in the place, don't I? What do you expect me to do when he comes in and sits down?

—Do you want me to take care of him for you?

—You keep out of this, Pearl shouted.

—Why? If you want him to leave you alone, why should I keep out of it?

—Yeah, and why do you think I don't get along with him now? Did you ever ask yourself that? Because Mother messed in our affairs and ruined everything. So you just keep out of it. I'll give Jeanette to Bob's family if you don't and go away where I'll never see any of you again. I'm so goddamned lonely I can't stand it any more.

—Well, why don't you live with him again?

—Yeah, why don't I?

—There are plenty of other guys.

—Not like him.

Pearl dried her eyes on her kimono and began to talk to Blackie as though she could not stop. Blackie listened to her with an expression of artificial gravity. She was treating him as an equal, and this was the way he wanted to be treated. She spoke to him as though he alone in the world could understand her, and he held his breath with attention as he had held his breath when he lay in the lower bunk at the school and listened to Whitey in the top bunk speaking to him in the same way, his attention metamorphosing every word spoken into a different and impersonal word heard. The closeness and the barrier were the same. But Pearl was confessing weakness, not strength, and as she went on talking he ceased to hear her and his impatience at her weakness grew.

—You ought to forget all about him and think about something else, he told her. Let's play cards.

—No, Pearl said. Not now.

—Well, what do you want to do?

—Nothing now. Anyway, I've got to get dressed for us to go to Mother's for dinner.

She kissed him so he would know she was not angry and pushed him toward the door. He waited in the hall a few seconds thinking that she might say something else to him, but she did not.

To go to Mother's for dinner he dressed in his new black shirt. The starched cloth irritated the nipples of his chest, and when he felt the nipples they were so sensitive to his touch that he wondered if he could have caught some disease. The baby rubbed against them as he carried her, and when he and Pearl arrived at Mother's he was glad to put the baby in the bed upstairs and leave Pearl alone with her. He went downstairs and found Gladys lying on the couch in the living room. She shouted a greeting to Blackie when he came in but she did not get up.

—Where's Caleb? he asked.

—I don't think he's coming, Gladys answered chewing gum.

—Why?

—I don't know. Ask Mother.

The three downstairs rooms ran parallel to the hall. The living room opened into the diningroom and the diningroom into the kitchen. Mother was in the kitchen cooking and sipping clear liquid from a mason ball jar. Blackie asked her where Caleb was.

—He didn't come, Mother answered. Those women he lives with wouldn't let him come. Besides, how'd I know you'd be here? You've got to learn, son, that you have certain responsibilities to others. And the sooner you learn it the better.

—That's your idea, he told her.

—Is that so? Mother inquired in an elegant voice. And just what are your ideas, may I ask?

—I can take care of myself, Blackie answered.

—Just like your sister Pearl, huh! All right, you stay with her. You two'll get along. I guess dog don't bite dog. I can see you don't need me any more. Go and set the table.

He went into the diningroom and put the plates around the table. They were new plates which he had not seen before, bordered with gold circles and painted flowers, particularly bright in the dark diningroom. When the table was set he went into the living room and smoked a cigarette sitting on the arm of the couch where Gladys was lying.

—Where'd the new dishes come from?

—I won them bowling, Gladys answered popping her gum.

—Got any more gum?

—Naw.

—You still on the bowling team?

—Yeah.

He went up to the bedroom and sat with Pearl who was

giving the baby her bottle so she would go to sleep. Pearl asked him to put out his cigarette because the smoke kept the baby awake. He put it out and sat on the top of the dresser, watching the baby go to sleep. Then Mother called from the kitchen that he had not put around the silver, and lighting another cigarette he went down to find the knives and forks and spoons.

—Well, I didn't know you smoked, Mother said ironically looking up from the stove.

He was standing by the kitchen table looking for the silver in the drawer. The mason ball jar was on the table. He lifted it and sniffed the contents.

—If I don't smoke will you give me a drink? he asked.

—Put that medicine down, Mother said. You'd better not let me catch you drinking until you're a grown man.

—I'm a man now, he answered arrogantly.

—You're not a man until you're twenty-one, Mother announced.

—I'm as much a man as I'll ever be, he announced back to her.

He went into the diningroom and after he had put around the silver stayed there tampering with a broken door hinge on a split veneer sideboard. When the meal began he was silent and resentful. He tried to get along with Mother but it was not right for her to tell him to do things and treat him as though he were a child. She had Gladys to help her and if Gladys did nothing it was Mother's own fault. As he helped his plate to meat he spilled gravy on his new black shirt and wiped it off with the tablecloth.

64

—Don't wipe that on my clean tablecloth, Mother said.

—It don't look so clean to me, Blackie said.

He continued to scrub at the grease stain with the table-cloth.

—Well, I washed it myself and it's cleaner than that shirt you've got on. Why don't you wear a nice white shirt instead of that ugly black thing anyway?

—Because I like this ugly black thing.

—Well, Mother said with sudden brightness, this is a reunion so we won't fuss. After all, we're having dinner together and we'll have a good time.

Mother and his sisters became cheerful immediately as though the squabbling meant nothing to them. Blackie nursed his grievance and did not speak unless he was spoken to. Mother had no right to say what she had said about his shirt without knowing why he wore it.

For dessert, Mother had made ice cream and baked a cake. And after dessert she told the children to go into the front room and amuse themselves while she did the dishes.

—What's changed her so? Blackie asked.

He nursed his resentment and felt allied with his sisters against Mother.

—Oh, I don't know, Pearl said. She's just that way.

—She's back there taking a drink, Gladys said. Sometimes I wonder why she don't just bring it in here and save herself a lot of walking.

Pearl brought Gladys' photograph album down from the mantel and showed Blackie the pictures which they had taken on his birthday in April. She sat on one arm of the

65

overstuffed mohair chair and Gladys flopped on the other. Blackie sat between them with the album on his lap. In the photographs everyone was clowning and pretending; if he had not taken some of the pictures Blackie would not have recognized them.

—Gee, look at you there!

He pointed to a photograph of Gladys. In the background the back porch ran uphill, and in front of it Gladys leaned forward at an angle, one knee bent, the other leg stretched out behind her, and her hands shielding her eyes like an Indian scout on the lookout.

Then they laughed at Mother as Blackie had photographed her when she was not ready, with one hand pulling down her corset and her tongue out wetting her lips. Of the whole family only Caleb, grinning into the camera, looked natural. Blackie did not like the photographs of himself and started to tear them out.

—Don't! Gladys screamed. It's my album and my pictures.

—Oh, leave them alone, Pearl said. They're cute.

Blackie gave in to his sisters because Mother came into the room and he wanted to seem to be having a good time while she was not there.

—Looking at pictures, huh? Mother said.

She flopped on the couch opposite the overstuffed chair, propped her feet up on the arm, and shut her eyes. Poking out her lower lip she blew her breath loudly up into the air to indicate how tired she was. She wanted the children to notice her but they continued to look at the photograph album.

Blackie whispered to Pearl and broke off in a giggle. Pearl laid her head down by Blackie's and giggled also. Eager and whispering, Gladys wanted to know what it was. They would not tell her for a while; but to keep her quiet Blackie explained that Mother had her feet propped up on the arm of the sofa in such a way that they could see straight up her dress. Gladys haw hawed. In her effort to place her head on a level with Blackie's she almost fell off the arm of the chair. Hearing the commotion, Mother opened her eyes and asked what was wrong. Her voice was so innocent that her three children collapsed in hysterics and writhed all over the dark overstuffed piece of furniture.

—Well, I don't want to pry into your secrets, Mother told them haughtily. It just seems to me that if there is anything funny you would want to tell me what it is.

Her face grew red. She propped herself on her elbows and swept her eyes about the room for the object of their mirth. Her eyes came to rest on herself as the only thing at which they looked as they writhed and laughed on the chair. Blackie's and Pearl's laughter had risen so high it was almost inaudible, but Gladys' had dropped to low asthmatical wheezes. Mother followed the direction of their eyes to the hem of her dress and haughtily put her feet down on the sofa.

—Well, I must say I don't see anything funny in that, she said patting the cushion behind her head and lying back.

67

She looked up at the ceiling, but they laughed all the more and she looked down at them again with fury.

—You needn't laugh at it, she snapped. You all came out of it.

Gladys sprang to her feet and her laughter dropped to a snarl.

—Well, as far as I'm concerned you can stuff me back up, she screamed.

Sobbing, she ran out of the room and up the stairs. Mother called after her:

—You behave. I want you all to behave when Ephraim gets here.

This announcement immediately sobered them.

—Is he coming? Pearl demanded. Is that why you're acting so sweet?

—You know we don't like him. Why do you let him come to see you when we're all here? Blackie demanded.

—He's my friend, Mother said.

—And you're always getting drunk with him, Pearl shouted. You're pretty good about telling me to forget my husband because he's no good, but you don't seem to forget your boyfriends.

—Just what do you wish to infer by that remark? Mother inquired.

—You know what I mean all right.

—Well, it's a fine thing when a mother has to ask her children who she can invite to her own house, Mother declared indignantly.

68

Blackie walked away into the diningroom. Mother shouted for him not to walk out of the room while she was talking, but he continued to the kitchen and shut the door. Through the closed door her voice reached him saying that she would have whomever she liked to her house whenever she pleased and that if her children did not like it they could all go live on the top floors of expensive duplexes.

On the kitchen table before the window the supper dishes were stacked, unwashed. The moon was up and through the window late light, not yet moonlight, fell onto the dirty dishes and Mother's jar of clear liquid. Angrily Blackie hit a cup with a brown ring of coffee in the bottom. The cup fell and the liquid spread out about it on the oilclothed table. He walked out of the grease staled kitchen onto the back porch and stood looking through the lattice at the patterns of dying light and shadow in the backyard. He wished he were still in the school, lying in his bunk after lights out listening to Whitey whisper to him in the moonlight. Strength and courage and indifference would be easy to practice there. Once he had seen Whitey go up to two boys who were rolling on the ground fighting, kick both of them in the head, and tell them to leave each other alone. And they had ceased fighting and gone about their work, respecting Whitey for what he had done and not hating him. But here, where everyone acted like a child and bickered and no one was in definite authority, what chance did strength and indifference have? He wished that Mother could have seen him the other night with Mabel, then she would realize he was a man. He decided to move to Pearl's house and have her write to the school to send his suitcase there. He would make money with Dusty and Hatchet and have about him the space and freedom which money creates. And he would buy a motorcycle and go where he was free to do whatever he imagined.

The doorbell rang. Blackie turned and faced the front of the house. Through the screen door he could see the silhouetted figure of a man and he knew that it was Ephraim. Ducking his head and sticking his right arm straight out in front of him, he charged. When his hand hit the screen door it flew open and struck the man full in the face and Blackie rushed past as the man fell. Mother came screaming into the hall and Ephraim cursed, but their words diminished beneath the echo of his footsteps up the pavement. Around the first corner he slowed to a walk and smiled. He wished that he had fought a real fight with Ephraim and he pictured himself on top of the older man beating his head against the porch and infuriating Mother who knocked her flowerpots off the banisters into the street when she tried to stop him.

Before the plate-glass window of a grocery store he stopped and looked at his reflection. His hair had fallen in his face and his shirt tail was out. He tucked in his shirt tail, hitched up his pants, and pushed his hair out of his face. As he lowered his hairoil stained fingers before his nose he smelled them and smiled again, sweet smelling and outlawed and evil now.

Along the streets the houses stood close together with only narrow alleyways between, block after block; and the large trees planted in the stretch of dirt between the sidewalk and the pavement mingled their leaves over the street in a continuous tunnel of green. The whole business of the family annoyed Blackie and he wanted to find the brothers and get together with them on a scheme for making money. You could not do anything with people like Pearl. He could take care of Bob for her if she would let him, but he would do what she asked. Yet for himself, he knew that he would never be so weak as to depend on any other person for his happiness. Sentimental, when he reached the playground he did not speak to anyone and went down to the wide field around the ball diamond where a group of kids were playing ball in the late summer light. Plop. He took a mitt and ball from one of them and threw the ball back and forth to another. The plop of the heavy ball against the leather of the mitt excited his desire for open conflict. Plop. He wanted to find Dusty and Hatchet and plot with them against someone whom they could attack and from whom they could steal money. Plop. Calling for the ball, he stood swinging his body from the hips, letting his buttocks drop from side to side as he shifted his weight from foot to foot, calling:

—Give it to me! Give it to me!

But the artificial excitement of the catch game did not satisfy him. He threw the glove back to the boy from whom he had taken it and walked toward the bathhouse. Run-

71

ning down the bank he ran into a spiderweb between two bushes and he was still pulling the spiderweb from his clothes and fingers when he entered the cement-floored concession building. The smell of hot dogs drowned the smell of chlorine from the pool and made him suddenly ravenously hungry. He ate three hot dogs at the lunch stand and asked the counterman if he had seen Dusty and Hatchet.

—They were here about an hour ago. Went home to supper, I guess.

With his mouth full of the last hot dog, still chewing and wiping the mustard from his fingers on his handkerchief, he went out to the narrow grandstand between the bathhouse and the pool. People sat beneath the awning of the grandstand in the daytime and watched the swimmers in the pool, but tonight the grandstand was deserted. No people were in swimming in the suppertime lull, and the evening sky was reflected in the unruffled water. But standing below him on the concrete walk which bordered the pool he saw Mabel talking to the blond man from the Cuban Villa. They were dressed in bathing suits and water glistened on their bare limbs. Mabel waved at Blackie, smiling brightly and jingling a bracelet on her wrist. He looked at her but did not answer.

—Come on down, Mabel called.

He sat on the wall of the grandstand facing away from her, and pretended that he did not hear. She had not entered his mind since morning and was not the object of his search in the park. He had come for something different.

But seeing her with the blond man made him angry. He feared that he was of no importance to her and that what she had done with him the other night she would do with the blond man tonight. As he heard her bangles jingle he could clearly picture her in bed with the blond and he wanted to go down and bash in the blond fellow's face; but he restrained himself, saying that it was no business of his for he did not care about Mabel; and he remained facing away from her, swinging his legs back and forth as he sat on the wall looking toward the building.

Mabel came up behind him and put her hands over his eyes.

—Go on, you'll get me all wet.

She felt like the sun standing behind him and touching his face.

—What's eating you? I'm the one who ought to be mad. You haven't been back to see me and I didn't know where to find you.

—It don't seem to be worrying you much.

She climbed over the low concrete wall, holding his shoulder to balance herself, and stood on the grass in front of him. He did not look at her until she tilted his chin up with her hand so he looked into her face. At that moment all the park lights came on, pale against the evening sky, dotting the whole landscape like lights reflected in a sheet of glass, and he saw Mabel's head close before him and large against the landscape, her forehead protruding and her hair, with drops of water in it, so fine that the shape of

73

her head was visible through it against the lights and sky. The dusk accentuated the artificiality of her lipstick and mascara, and made her teeth glow white and crooked when she smiled.

—You're jealous, she said.

—If you think I'm jealous go on back to him and find out.

—I have to go out with older boys who can buy me things, but I don't like them the way I like you.

—What makes you think I wouldn't buy you things?

—Well, you haven't. And besides, I wouldn't want you to.

—You'd better go back to your boyfriend.

—He's nobody. He brought me out, but you can take me home if you want to. Don't you want to?

—It's all right with me. But I'm not going to sit here and watch you with him.

—That's all right. I'm going to get dressed now and you can meet me somewhere else. Where'll you be?

—Up at the playground.

—Oh, I don't want to come up there. Meet me at one of the swings by the lake. All right?

—What about him?

—Him? Oh, he has to go to work.

The path was deserted as he walked around the lake to the far side of the playground and up wide grassthreaded stone steps at the top of which two empty urns stood against the sky. The top of the hill was flat and he seemed to be

74

walking toward the bare sky, but when he reached the top of the steps the new dark before him was dotted with the silhouettes of people and the bright tips of cigarettes. The rest of the park might be deserted at night but the playground, emptied of the children of the day, was a complete city. People of all ages stood a few feet from each other in the dark, and Blackie walked through them, past the sliding board and swings all the way to the authors' monument, the clump of dried cedar trees and the wooden hand-pushed merry-go-round at the far end. But he did not find Dusty and Hatchet and he retraced his steps down the hill again to the end of the lake where he stood beneath a magnolia tree tossing a magnolia cone he picked up from the earth.

Between each of the lamps which circled the lake there was a swing in the dark. In each swing someone was sitting, a man or a man and a woman. The evening was perfectly quiet. Dust had settled on the water of the lake which looked like soft rubber, and no one came near the lake until Mabel appeared around the far curve passing through the dark from circle of light to circle of light and peering unself-consciously at the people seated in the swings between. Blackie stood beneath the magnolia tree and waited for her. He did not start to meet her and did not even walk out on the path when he heard the slow crunch of her feet nearing him across the gravel.

—Blackie, is that you?

—Yeah.

75

—Well, for Christ sake, why don't you say so? she asked cheerfully. This is a goddamned big lake, you know. I been looking for you all the way around it.

Smiling she took his arm. He flipped his cigarette into the street and walked along with her without responding to her grasp on his arm.

—I'd like to meet that guy from the Cuban Villa, he said.

—Blackie, are you still thinking about him?

—Who said I was thinking about him? I said I'd like to meet him.

—Well, what are you so cross about? Mad because I went swimming?

Her insignificance in relation to his desire for independence overcame him.

—I'm going by the Boss Avenue dance hall to look for a couple of friends of mine. Do you want to come? he asked.

—Sure, she answered. Why do you think I met you?

The dance hall had been a skating rink and was on the second floor of a garage. A crowd of kids Blackie had known at school and in the park were crowded around the refreshment booth and he stopped to talk to them.

—Say, ain't you Jim's wife? the counterman asked Mabel.

—No, she called to him, I ain't.

She left Blackie and went to the rest room. But when she came back she spoke to the counterman again.

—Yeah, I'm Jim's wife, she said, but I don't associate with him any more.

76

Blackie gave no sign that he did not know she was married. He led her out onto the dance floor and put his arm around her. They danced for a few minutes to *Did You Ever See a Dream Walking?* grinding out of a juke-box in the middle of a mica-splattered bandstand at the far end of the room. Then Blackie asked:

—Where's your husband?

—Oh, I don't know, Mabel said. Out of the state somewhere. He was a stomachturner. All I ever got from him was trouble. But don't you worry, he won't come back in the state.

When the record was over Blackie led Mabel to one of the benches which lined the wall and left her with a group of his friends while he went to buy them a couple of beers with the change he had left from the five dollars. As he walked back across the dance floor with the two bottles in his hands he felt Mabel watching him and saw himself in her eyes. He was quick to imitate and improve on mannerisms which he admired and he knew that he walked in the muscle-bound way Whitey had walked, shifted his cigarette between his lips the way James Cagney shifted a cigarette, and smiled the sarcastic way the blond man at the Cuban Villa had smiled. When he reached Mabel he handed her a beer and ran his eyes down her figure as he always had seen certain men run their eyes down the figures of women. Then he threw his cigarette away and exhaled the smoke through his nose.

—I'm glad we came here, he said. Nice place.

77

And he recognized the passion in her voice as she replied:

—I'm glad we came, too. I don't like the Cuban Villa. That's where I met my husband.

While they were dancing the second time, Blackie saw Dusty and Hatchet enter the dance hall. He waved to them and led Mabel across to the bench and introduced the brothers to her. The brothers said that they wanted to talk to Blackie privately a minute. Importantly Blackie took leave of Mabel and followed them along the wall. He stood before them, a hand on a shoulder of each, and smiled.

—Where were you the other night? Dusty asked.

—Sorry I didn't get by the park. You see, I ran into Mabel.

—Where'd you run into her?

—At the Cuban Villa.

—Yeah, we heard you were there, Hatchet said.

—Yeah, I went by looking for Crip. Why, don't you like it?

He took his hands from the brothers' shoulders and narrowed his eyes.

—Crip don't ever go to the Cuban Villa. He hates his brother like hell, Hatchet said.

—He sells liquor for him, don't he? Blackie asked.

—Not any more, Dusty said. He buys that liquor over on the south side for a quarter and sells it here for fifty cents, and if his brother ever catches him he'll beat hell out of him for it.

78

—O.K. How was I to know that?

—We're telling you, Hatchet told him.

—You're not telling me nothing, Blackie said.

—No use getting mad, Dusty told him. It's just that we had a run in with those guys at the Cuban Villa. You'll understand when we tell you about it. But if you're going to be in with us on something we got in mind you'd better not go around the Cuban Villa. There's money in it.

—That sounds better, Blackie said. I'll talk to you about it in a few minutes. I've got to go dance now.

The music had started again. He led Mabel out onto the dance floor, singing in her ear the song on the jukebox.

—What were you talking about to those guys? Mabel asked.

—Nothing.

—Are they friends of yours?

—Why?

—I've heard about them over at the Cuban Villa. They got in trouble there and the guys who run the place are on the watchout for them. Don't let them get you into trouble.

—What kind of trouble? Blackie asked.

—I don't know, Mabel said. Just trouble.

When the record finished they joined Dusty and Hatchet back at the bench. Blackie stood between the brothers, his arms about their shoulders, looking at Mabel. His face was covered with sweat and his large features glowed with a dark intensity. His eyes flashed when he looked at Mabel or winked at Dusty or Hatchet, and though he directed all his remarks to the boys on either side of him, intimately and in-sinuatingly, he widened his mouth and narrowed his eyes and looked at Mabel as he spoke so everyone would know of his intimacy with her. The brothers played up to him, re-marking when he winked that one eye was still open, and laughing with approval when he wiggled his body in imita-tion of the desirability he saw in Mabel.

Soon they were the center of a group gathered about the bench.

—Why do you wear a black shirt, Blackie? someone asked.

All evening he had waited for that question, but now the words came from a stranger and faded past him without significance in the warm air of the dance hall.

—Because he's a Jack of Spades, Dusty said.

—No, because his name's Blackie, Mabel laughed.

The crowd joined in her laughter and Blackie leaned forward and took Mabel's jaw in his hand to kiss her. His mourning for Whitey was his secret, even though he had told his friends, and he did not mind as much as he had thought he would. He was almost pleased. And amid whistles and laughter he led Mabel out onto the dance floor again and pressed his body against hers.

—It's too hot in here, Mabel whispered. Let's go back to my room.

Threatening her amorously, he led her from the dance floor. At the entrance Dusty stopped them and took Blackie aside.

—Where are you going? Dusty asked. I thought you were going to talk to us.

—All right, Blackie said. Baby, wait for me a minute.

He went with the brothers into the men's toilet and standing against the wall they told him their plan.

By a remark from Crip, Dusty and Hatchet had learned where Crip's brother who ran the Cuban Villa kept his car, in a garage on Crescent Avenue. They planned to steal the car, which had a stepped-up motor, and sell it somewhere in the south of the state, probably Macon. Dusty knew some people there who would know how to sell it. The police, they figured, would not be notified and there was nothing to worry about if the job were well planned. The car would go so fast there would be no trouble getting away with it even if they were chased, and there would be little chance of that as no one suspected them, not even Crip. Now Blackie would understand why they had been upset when they learned that he had been to the Cuban Villa with Mabel, but perhaps it was better if he were friendly there for it would place them further from suspicion.

Blackie heard them to the finish without interrupting. But he was disgusted. Dusty did most of the talking but Hatchet put in an excited sentence every now and then. With gestures and voices the brothers showed their self-importance just when Blackie felt that by silence and cessation of all gesture they should have indicated that the subject of which they spoke was worthy of respect. They might as well have told him that they were going to Chicago or New York and double cross the gangsters there because the gangsters would not be able to send the police after them, and he told them that he thought so. He had heard guys who hung out at the Cuban Villa refer to the Fair Street jail as their second home. They were tougher than the police and took the police in stride. He was going to be on their side, not against them, if he had anything to do with them, and the brothers would drop their plan at once if they knew what was good for them.

—What do you mean? Hatchet demanded.

—I mean that I thought you had a plan to get some money, not a free ride to the boneyard.

—But you can't back out now that you know our plan.

—That's your worry not mine.

Hatchet was angry, but Dusty quieted him.

—O.K., Blackie, he said, but you're wrong.

—It's not me who's wrong, Blackie said.

He turned and walked away from them, out of the toilet; and as the door closed behind him he heard Hatchet's angry voice call that the more he saw of people the better he liked dogs.

He took Mabel's arm and walked toward the corner with her in angry silence.

—Shall we take a streetcar uptown? she asked. My feet are killing me.

—Uptown?

—Yeah, you're coming to my room with me, ain't you?

He had forgotten that she had invited him to go to bed

with her again. He looked at her with a new self-confidence and pride as they waited at the streetcar stop, and as they rode uptown on the streetcar she assumed a new importance. Desire grew in his mind and he could hardly wait until he was alone with her in the hotel room. In no other place in the city had he found the mystery and excitement to which he wished to ally himself: the city was like a pair of tight pants binding and restraining him whenever he tried to imitate with his body the dark movements which he felt in his imagination.

Over the rattle of the wheels on crosstracks he heard thunder in the sky and said that he thought it was going to rain.

—No, I don't think so, Mabel said placing her hand in his on the straw seat between them and scratching his palm with her fingernail. If it don't rain on the first of dog days it don't rain until they're over.

—Do you believe that stuff?

He was thinking that perhaps he did not need to ally himself to strength but to separate himself from weakness and stupidity.

—No, Mabel said. But I'd be willing to bet you that it won't rain until they're over.

And that with Mabel he would be quite separate from fools like the brothers.

—And if it had rained the first day, Mabel said, I'd bet you that it would rain every day until they're over.

When he kissed her in her room at the hotel, she said that she loved him.

He was pleased and surprised. It never had occurred to him that love was connected with this. He had played with little girls in garages and beneath houses since he could remember. In the park at night he had gone as far with them, playing around the world, as he had gone with Mabel. It had been an adventure, but it was the opposite of what he thought of as love. Love was something great and strong, unconnected with actions which were near and seen and named. Love was an escape from everyday life, not a part of it. Looking at Mabel as though he never had seen her before, he ran his hands down her soft firm body before he answered. He did not really believe it, yet it made him incredibly happy to reduce love to what stood before him to be looked at and touched with his hands.

—I love you, too, he said.

After they had been to bed he got up for a cigarette and walked to the window to think more about love. Standing with his fist on his rump, he looked down into the back street. On the sidewalk below, narrower than a hotel corridor, a woman in an orange dress was walking a dog in and out of the pink glow of the neon sign which flashed: In and Out All Day—10¢—: and in and out of the view from the window. Beyond the parking lot a small shack against the back of a large building appeared and disappeared with the flashes of the sign. He put out his cigarette, pulled down the shade and went back to bed.

In the near dark of the room everything was colorless. Lying on the bed, the entire length of his body touching

Mabel, he enjoyed the touch of her body and heard her whisper that the smell of his neck was wonderful. From another room the clink of glasses and the trill of laughter came in spasmodically on the still air, entering the silence like lights entering the dark, and once a breeze flapped the windowshade ecstatically. He put his hands behind his neck and raised his head to look at the window. But he was too content lying in bed thinking about love: with love everything would be all right, he could go his own way and make his life strong and good despite the weak and foolish ways of others; he would have his fate in his own hands; he would not have to be a part of the meaninglessness which surrounded him.

And lying back, his shoulder touching Mabel's shoulder and her face against his neck, he went to sleep again in the dark.

CHAPTER 4

Every day for two weeks Blackie went to see Mabel in her room at the hotel.

Filled with a morning joy of knowing where he wanted to go and what he wanted to do, he crossed the dim black and white tile floor of the lobby and mounted the stairs behind the recently installed elevator to the third floor. In the brown and tan hallway he knocked on Mabel's door.

When the transom, held in place by a latch and chain, fell open he saw the room in the daylight for the first time. Now that it was light he no longer felt like a clandestine lover and the fear which he had felt of being suddenly denounced was metamorphosed into a desire to find out everything he could about happiness and this girl who preferred him to all the grown men she knew in the city.

Opposite the door the window looked out through the black skeleton of the fire escape onto the sky, bright blue and cloudless, above the brick and tarpaper backs of office buildings in the sunshine. The sunshine streamed in through the soft wood of the windowframe and across the pumice colored clothes closet which lined the left wall as far as the sink in the corner and reflected on Mabel's hair and the row of grease spots along the flowered wallpaper above the bed where people had sat and leaned their heads.

Mabel always sat on the bed, facing the door with her back to the window, and when Blackie arrived she usually was polishing or filing her fingernails, the bottle of polish balanced precariously on the white bedspread beside her, and without getting up she would shout for him to come in. She smiled as she brushed the polish on with a kind of clipped delicacy, spreading the red lacquer the length of her tiny fingernails in three strokes, inspecting them to see if the lacquer were smooth, and if it were not wiping the lacquer off on a towel and starting again.

The smallness and strangeness of the room, the bed with its spread the color of the white workhorse at the farm school, the basin in the corner which dripped continually as water drips over the spillway from a stream into a pool, and Mabel dressed only in her slip and smiling at him from where she sat propped against the foot of the bed, filled Blackie with happiness and excitement. Mabel was as exciting and mysterious to him as the sea of which he had heard but which he had never seen. There was one chair in the room but he always sat on the bed with Mabel. When he arrived she put away her cosmetics and devoted herself entirely to him, and he was entirely occupied with her excitement and mystery.

88

Hour by hour passed without his thinking consciously of the image he wanted to live up to. His thoughts and feelings were drawn entirely outside himself and absorbed in the adventure of discovery which he was making. Sitting or lying on the bed with her, he was continually aware of Mabel's awareness of him and of the ways in which she appreciated his presence, feeling his arms, kissing his neck, looking at him as though she saw something wonderful in his face and asking him to come lie at her end of the bed when he sat at the far end and looked at her. Then, lying close to her and looking up at the ceiling, he asked questions and his interest grew until he could no longer contain it and they made love.

They made love and talked and drank beer. Sometimes Mabel's friend, a girl with dyed dark red hair who lived down the hall, came in and spoke to Mabel; and Blackie liked knowing that the girl knew about them. But Mabel preferred to be alone and the girl never stayed long. The first day Blackie brought his bathing suit and they went to the park and swam. But Mabel said that she did not like going to the park where there were so many people and after the first day they deserted the park for the hotel. They sat on the bed and drank beer and talked about what they would do together, how Blackie would get a job as an automobile mechanic when he finished school and they would go away together.

But by the beginning of the second week Blackie discovered that he had come to the limit of the things he could talk about with Mabel. He was still full of excitement, but his questions were all confronted with the same answers over again as though there were no new knowledge to discover. So on his way up town the next morning he tried to get a job in a garage. He was too full of excitement to do nothing, and if there were no new things to be talked about there were things to do. He could do anything that he wanted to with machinery and if someone would just give him the chance he could learn all about repairing automobiles in no time. But, although between North Avenue and Houston Street he stopped in every garage and filling station, no one even listened seriously to his request. He was too young and there were too many mechanics out of work. He arrived at the hotel in a belligerent mood and with a growing feeling of disillusion he sensed that the same limitation was in Mabel, that she desired him more than he desired her and that he did not have to take her desires into consideration any more than he did the desires of the people he had ceased to consider his friends.

He tested his new power tentatively at first, arriving at the hotel earlier or later than Mabel expected him to see if she would welcome him at any time, and when this succeeded, more boldly, leaving the room for a moment and remaining away for an hour. If he said that he was going around the corner to get a couple of bottles of cold beer, he walked down to Decatur Street and looked at the knives and guns and gold rings in the windows of loan shops, or as far as the brewery on Courtland Street and talked with a fellow he knew who

90

was loading trucks there that summer. When he returned he bought the beer around the corner from the hotel and carried it up to the room and made no mention of his absence. Mabel complained that he had been away a long time. But she did not demand an explanation. She accepted him as a man with the sort of business men have which is no concern of women, and he accepted her evaluation.

In the evenings he no longer went to the park. He did not want to see the brothers; it was one of his ideas that it was not honorable to pretend friendliness for an enemy, and he avoided even the houses of boys and girls in the neighborhood where he might see Dusty and Hatchet. He had a new group of friends in the cafés around the hotel, boys who worked as ushers in theaters or bellhops in hotels or who simply hung around because it was summer. But they had no real place in his heart. Most of the evenings he went home so that Mother and Pearl would not become suspicious that he was away from both of the houses all the time. He spent his evenings about one of the two houses talking to Pearl or Mother and repairing, or simply taking apart and putting back together, everything which could be taken apart. Once or twice he felt a vague misgiving that Whitey would not have approved of his spending so much time around women, but he put aside his misgivings and went about his work in the houses.

In the later part of the week, however, his restlessness increased. He began to prefer being at the brewery plant to being at the hotel. Indoors there was not enough outlet for his energy. There was no scope for action in the time he spent with Mabel. Each afternoon with her passed in such softness and contentment that he began to fear softness and contentment as most men fear violence. When Mabel did not want to do the things he wanted to do, he suspected her now of consciously opposing his attempt to live up to his ideal, of admiring the wrong things in him and of considering as bad all the traits of which he was proud. She thought that he should spend all his time making love to her and listening to her talk about how wonderful his neck smelled and betting her that she could not tell whether or not he had been drinking beer just by smelling it. If he said that he wanted to go out she said that he ought to wait until evening and take her dancing. She wanted to talk and she talked about things which were of interest only to women, about what the girl down the hall had said and how she looked today and what she was going to do tomorrow, until he suspected her of deceiving him, of being exactly the opposite of what he had thought her to be. But he saw through her deception. He began to watch her as an enemy from the time he arrived at the hotel in the morning until he left in the afternoon and to chronicle against her with growing calculation all the offenses he found.

He was sitting in the sill of the open window and could see the grass and the few sunflowers with ragged leaves and heavy yellow blossoms motionless in the fierce heat at the side of the cinder parking lot. Mabel was at the dresser looking in the mirror, putting something on her face and telling him about the white circles she had gotten around her eyes the first of the summer when she had put cotton pads soaked in cucumber lotion over her eyelids after she returned from swimming, knowing only that it was an astringent and not that it was a bleach. She laughed at herself, and the story made her sound like a fool. At first Blackie had thought when she told stories on herself that she had some ulterior motive, but he had never found one. Now he concluded that she had no self-respect.

He was leaning against the head of the bed after they had been playing cards on the mattress, looking at her leaning against the foot, the dark curve of her breast visible under the lace of her slip and the dark curve of her thighs slipshadowed against the tangled spread. In a self-dramatizing voice she was telling him about her husband. He had found a dime strip of photographs of her husband in the small top drawer of the dresser when he got out the deck of cards to play rummy. He respected the looks of the man in the photographs, darkfaced and hollowcheeked, but he had been annoyed and shoved the pictures to the back of the drawer after he held them up and Mabel, looking over her shoulder, told him who it was. When he returned to the bed he could see the pictures where they had fallen out of the back of the drawer down in the dust against the floorboard beneath the dresser. He did not tell Mabel, but when the game was over he looked down and saw the strip of pictures again and asked where she and her husband had met. She always answered whatever he asked. She had told

93

him how she quarreled with her family about marrying and how she left home in spite of them. For that reason she had been too proud to return home after her separation. And now she told him how she had met her husband at the Cuban Villa a week before they were married and had gone with him to Alabama the day after the wedding. Her husband had led her to believe that he was a traveling salesman, but when they reached Anniston she had discovered that he was in charge of a gang of pimply faced kids soliciting subscriptions for a national magazine. He made almost no money and when she refused to give him her savings he cried. All the time he got drunk or cried, and one morning he had *gone to the toilet* lying in bed simply because he was too lazy to get up. That had finished him for her.

This story almost finished her for Blackie. Now that she had dropped her modesty, he discovered that Mabel talked more coarsely, with more reference to physical functions and with less delicacy, than any boy he had ever known. He liked vulgar words and sly inferences, but he did not like the constant references she made to what people did and her replies annoyed him as much as her refusal to reply would have.

In answer to his anger she came up to his end of the bed and, laying her face in his armpit, asked what she had done that was wrong. When her body was against his he knew that he had been wrong in ascribing mystery to her. There was no mystery in her. There was no spirit. She was coarse, and her love for him was only what he saw, only

94

physical desire. She had never appreciated his possibilities of strength and greatness. In anger, he made love to her, trying to impress his anger on her as deeply and as painfully as possible, but when his desire was gone his anger remained.

He lay on the bed waiting for her to return from the bathroom down the hall, his hands folded under his head, his elbows akimbo, and every now and then he slipped one hand out from beneath his head and held his cigarette across his bare chest to the edge of the bed and flicked off the ashes with his little finger. He felt disgusted as though he had done something which he should not have done. When he had wanted to make love to her his desire had seemed the important thing, but now that he was satisfied he himself, as he was all the time without desire, seemed of more import. She had, at least temporarily, taken away from him the identity of which he was proud and made him like herself, with no purpose in life beyond sloth and pleasure. She had used his desire to bind him to her and make him spend his life as she spent hers, day after day, in doing things which were not manly. But he was too strong for her. In disgust, he rose from the bed and readied himself to leave.

When she returned to the room, however, he felt differently. He was standing at the basin in the corner and washing. The afternoon sun streamed into the room reflecting patterns of sunlight and water, transparent with clear waves, over his wet hands and onto the ceiling. She came up behind and kissed him on the neck, timidly, not possessively but as though she respected his independence. He was annoyed that she should make herself so pleasant when he had decided to leave.

—Blackie, can I ask you something? she asked.

—What? he said drying his hands.

His voice sounded harsh and he was glad. That would put her on the defensive. But when he turned and saw her standing in the sunshine he was sorry that he had spoken harshly. Her face was changed more than her voice. All her features were softer and the need of her softness for his strength seemed to have softened her eyes.

But he did not forget to chronicle her weakness against her as she told him what she wanted. She went to the dresser and brought back a length of gold chain with a locket on the end. She was going to have the chain made into a bracelet and wear it on her wrist instead of about her neck, which was not fashionable, and there would be enough chain left over for another bracelet. She wondered if he would wear a chain also. It would be like wearing wedding rings, only no one else would know what it meant, and they could have a jeweler solder the chains on their wrists so they could not take them off.

—Only maybe you think wearing a bracelet is sissy, she said softly.

—There won't be anything sissy about my wearing one, he answered firmly.

Leaning against the doorframe and smoking a cigarette he watched her from the door as she got ready to go out.

He liked the idea of the gold chain almost more than she did, but he added it to his grievances, and when she was ready to go he dropped his cigarette and stepped on it and followed her as though he were not taken in at all.

The lights in store windows and the neon signs over the sidewalks were burning although the sky and streets were still light. At a jeweler's next to the viaduct Blackie and Mabel had the bracelets soldered on their wrists, and afterwards they stood self-consciously on the viaduct feeling the chains and looking down at the railroad tracks which ran through the middle of the city. It seemed to Blackie that everyone on the warm crowded sidewalk must be aware of the chain on his wrist, but on the way back to the hotel they met Caleb and Caleb did not notice.

Caleb was on his way to a movie.

—Let's go with him, Blackie said.

—You don't really want to go to a movie, do you? asked Mabel.

—Sure, Blackie said. Come on.

He led her to the theater, pretending to be unaware of her desire to return to the hotel, and borrowed money from her for the tickets. When they came out of the aircooled theater into the summer night he suggested that they have a mugglewuggle.

—Wouldn't you rather have a beer? asked Mabel.

—No, I don't feel like a beer, Blackie told her. You don't want a beer either. Come on.

Decisively he led the way into a soda fountain and

97

ordered three caramel walnut ice cream sundaes. When they had eaten the sundaes and come out onto the street again he told Caleb to walk them to the hotel and he would walk Caleb part way home. At the alley Mabel took Blackie aside and asked if he did not want to come up to her room for a while. He told her that he did not, then departed.

Saturday the sky clouded over black at noon and thunder rumbled low and musical. As Blackie arrived at the hotel a fiery lingam split the sky and was followed by a bang as though a building had fallen in the street. In her room he found Mabel lying on the bed, touching neither foot nor head, frightened by the thunderstorm.

—Close the window and come lie down, she commanded.

—Why? he asked. It ain't going to rain.

—It's going to lightning, she told him fearfully. Close the window, Blackie.

He had come armed with the guitar. By not thinking of Mabel through the morning he had forgotten the emotion of the afternoon before when she suggested that he wear the bracelet and he had remembered only her weakness, the stories about her husband and her trip to Alabama, and her attempt to tie him to her weaknesses.

—The lightning can't hurt you, he told her. It's already struck when you see the flash.

—Well, that must be a lot of comfort to the people who've been killed by it, Mabel said crossly.

She turned her face toward the wall and pretended to ignore him, but when he took the guitar from the dresser she turned back and told him not to come near the bed with the guitar because the metal strings attracted the lightning. He sat in the chair with his feet on the bed and played her a song. When he finished he played another. It was as though he were unable to put the guitar down, as though he suddenly felt himself vulnerable and unprotected before her fear of the storm, and song after song he played while all the weaknesses she had exposed him to since he had known her flowed through his mind. After each song he asked if she liked it and she answered yes each time, but he knew that she wanted him to stop playing and lie on the bed beside her. At last, when he had built up enough resentment in his mind against her, he felt safe enough to lay the guitar on the floor, take off his shoes, and lie down beside her. But as soon as he was on the bed she put her fingers on his arm to convince herself of his closeness and he avoided her again, saying:

—Here's another one, see if you know it.

Slowly, perfectly, endlessly, he whistled. The thunder and lightning stopped without a drop of rain having fallen. The clouds blew over leaving the sky light and hot again. Mabel lay so close to him that he could feel her breast rising and falling as she breathed, and when he took a deep breath at the end of one song to begin whistling another his nostrils were filled with the odors of her perfume and body. Still, he whistled until Mabel turned away from him, resigned; then he stopped and asked her what was the matter. He had promised himself that he would wait for her to make the first advance, and when instead of answering she turned to him again and kissed him he did not respond until she pulled away indignant at his indifference. Then he grabbed her and kissed her so hard that his teeth hit against hers. She pulled away, and he thought: What a stubborn fool, when I don't kiss her she pouts and when I do she pulls away.

Having put himself in the position of benefactor, he made love to her, but there was no pleasure in it. Fostered by the sun's heat his passion had shot up rapidly, but having no roots it had withered as rapidly away. The end of his being angry was that he became hungry.

—Ain't there anything to eat here? he asked remembering how Mabel had described to him the raw eggs and milk, food to put lead in your pencil as she called it, which she had kept on the windowsill in winter.

—No, Mabel sniffed sleepily.

—Let's go out and eat then, Blackie suggested.

—In a little, Mabel grunted. Let's sleep a little first.

Impelled by her opposition he put his feet to the floor and sat on the edge of the bed. He seemed not to have changed her at all but to have been caught in the trap, as though the whole purpose of her lying on the bed in fear of the thunder had been to make him make love. Suddenly he wanted to leave and be free of her completely. But he knew that she would complain if he wanted to go out and he decided to lose his temper before she had a chance to lose hers, so he would seem the injured party after his departure.

—You ain't hungry, huh? he insisted.

—Yes, but I'm sleepy, she drawled. Wait a little and I'll go with you.

He dressed and stood at the door of the room staring at her until she sensed it and opened her eyes. Seeing him at the door she asked:

—You going out now?

—Unless you think you can stop me.

She seemed so wrapped up in her own feelings lying there, so unaware of his thoughts.

—Not if you don't want me to, she sighed and closed her eyes again.

—Oh, yes you do, he accused. You think that just because you make love to me you can make me do anything you want me to. But making love ain't nothing to me.

—Oh, for God's sake act yourself, Mabel sighed with exasperation. For days you've been acting the mysterious tough guy and it don't fit you. I love you because you're fun to make love to and because you're full of feeling for a boy. I've never known anyone so full of feeling. But suddenly you seem to be ashamed of it. All day long you've been acting like everything we did disgusted you. When you're older you'll learn to like what you do and to forget your kid ideas about what life's going to be like.

—Yeah? Blackie demanded.

—Yeah, Mabel said. And maybe you'll learn that you're ugly when you stand off and sneer at me like that. I guess you think it makes you look manly, but it just makes you look like a snotty faced little kid. Why don't you be yourself?

—Yeah? he sneered. You think you can get by with saying things like that because you're older than me. Well, I'm a lot older than you'll ever be and I've already lived a lot more than you'll ever live because you're just a snotty faced little whore.

—Why you little son of a bitch, she shouted propping herself up on her elbow.

He leapt at her, caught her arm and twisted it up behind her back before she knew what he was doing.

—Stop it, you're hurting me, she cried.

—Take it back!

—I didn't say anything to take back.

—You called my mother a bitch. Take it back or I'll break your arm.

—I take it back. I didn't think about your mother. You know I didn't think about your mother. You're just mean, that's all you are, mean.

—Sure I'm mean, didn't you know I'm mean? he boasted.

He glared down at her while she rubbed the wrist of the hand he had twisted and sympathetically examined its pained flesh.

—Well, you'll never get a chance to be mean to me again. Go on out and get something to eat and never come back.

—Bargain!

He slammed the door and stalked down the stairs and

out of the hotel. As he entered the street from the alley he remembered that he did not have any money and that if he was going to eat he would have to borrow some or go home to Mother's and see what was in the icebox. There was almost never any food except milk at Pearl's. He turned and walked down Ivy Street looking into the windows of the cafés to see if there was anyone from whom he could borrow two bits for a sandwich and beer.

On Ivy Street he ran into Caleb. Caleb took a package of cigarettes out of his pocket as soon as he saw Blackie and offered him a cigarette so Blackie would know that he was smoking.

—Lend me two bits, Blackie said as he took one.

—I ain't got but a dime, Caleb told him.

—O.K., let's both get a candy bar.

They walked to the corner and bought two candy bars in a drugstore. Then they came out onto the sidewalk and stood eating and staring at the passing traffic.

—Have you been to see Mabel? Caleb asked.

Blackie looked at him.

—Yeah. Why?

—She's nice, Caleb said.

—Oh, it's good stuff, Blackie told him confidentially. But she's not worth the trouble of staying around. No girl's worth it. The minute they think they've got you they start trying to change you and it's not worth it. The thing to do is get what you want from them and leave. Remember that when your pecker gets hard.

103

—I know a fellow who says he laid Mabel, Caleb revealed in returned confidence.

—Who? Blackie asked.

—His name is Albert. You don't know him. He never hangs around the park. But I just saw him on Carnegie Way going to get a job with a wrecking company tearing down houses for a project over on Techwood near where Mother lives.

—Show me where, Blackie said.

—Are you going to get in a fight with him? Caleb asked.

Blackie put his hand on his little brother's head and tousled his hair.

—Naw, kid, he said. I'm going to get myself a job.

CHAPTER 5

With his hands low on his hips, Blackie stood beside an empty trash barrel at the curb. Behind him in a portable toolhouse straddling the curb, the workmen were changing into their workclothes. He could hear the voices of the men sleepy and grumbling. Most of them were much older than he and he stood a little apart. They thought he was seventeen anyway, and he felt older now that he had a job. Summer always had been the time to do nothing but wander in the park all day and chase girls through the back alley or stand in the circles of light under street lamps at night while bats flew down into the light and back up into the dark sky. But now he would work all year round, like any man, twelve months a year. The idea was endless and fascinating. He looked at the dumptruck across the street waiting to take away the wood and plaster of the rotten houses when they were demolished and wished that he could drive it. All about him along the street and among the houses grew heavy low trees full of green leaves, and in the distance office buildings were white with early morning sun. As he stood, conscious of the sun on his body and on his upper arms, heavy and melonlike, that filled and stretched the torn off sleeves of his shirt, a truck appeared from the shade of a side street into the sunlight. The red cab came up the hill and leveled while the corrugated chromium boxcar of the trailer slanted downhill behind it. Then the cab disappeared on the other side of the street, the great silver body of the trailer leveled for a moment, larger than the mound of earth beneath it, and crept slowly down the hill, all its powerful weight held back by the small red cab. The driver was visible but an instant, his face impassive and strong, his arm resting along the edge of the window. But when the truck and the trailer were out of sight, Blackie remembered the driver and envied him.

The workmen were dressed. They stood about him beneath the cloudless blue sky and watched the heat slowly descending over the distant office buildings to the deserted streets and houses. Blackie wanted to talk to the driver of the dumptruck, but he did not know which of the men was he. Most of the workers were large and crude with round red eyes and open voices. A few were worn out and thin. There was only one boy Blackie's age, Albert, and when the foreman shouted for them to set to, Blackie hit the boy on the shoulder and shouted:

—Come on, Albert, let's go.

They stopped for dinner at noon and ate in the shade of

a cottonwood tree among the half demolished houses. The houses were so old and rotten that they fell apart. It was more difficult to keep them from falling on you than to pull them down, and during the morning a man's leg had been crushed beneath a roof which had fallen without warning and brought the chimney down with it. The man had moaned like a wounded animal until the other workmen freed him and he was taken away to the hospital. The workmen talked of the accident as they sat under the large tree and ate dinner. The men ate sandwiches and tomatoes, and drank an ice cold and sweating quart bottle of beer. Removing the cap, they left the beer bottle in the sack and passed the wet sack back and forth drinking out of it. The large whiskeyeyed man who had gone for the beer ate half a sandwich at one bite, moving his whole jaw up and down as he chewed, or half a tomato, sucking at the other half to catch the juice; his hands were numb from the heavy work and he picked up the food with them awkwardly, as though they were tongs. He kept offering the beer to Blackie, telling him not to be bashful if he was thirsty. Blackie drank several times and talked to the whiskeyeyed man as he ate. When they finished, the man put all the empty sacks and papers into one bag and threw it on the ground where it lay until the wind blew the papers out and scattered them separately among the frames and foundations of the half demolished houses.

After the clear sharp morning, the heat bore down through the oppressive afternoon as though the air were solidifying into hot concrete on every surface of his body. The thermometer in the shade at the side of the toolhouse reached ninety-eight degrees. Yet Blackie was not annoyed by the heat. In the effort of combating the solitude which he felt, he held back from himself the admission of any small annoyances as though he were incapable of feeling them. He worked with a seemingly invulnerable contentment through the shadowless afternoon.

It was still hot when they quit work at five. The workmen got in old automobiles and drove away. Blackie walked to Pearl's house. He was covered with sweat, plaster and wooddust, and when Pearl came in with the baby and called to him he was in the tub. She called through the bathroom door that Mother was going to watch the baby for the night and asked if he wanted to go to a movie with her. He answered that he did, but while Pearl was in the tub taking her bath he finished dressing and went out. He did not want to be with women; he still was filled with a baffled and unrecognized resentment against a feminine world in which no mystery remained except that of being a man. Alone and without any planned destination he left the house and circled slowly toward the green heart of the city, his invulnerability guarding his solitude like a man with a club guarding a sacred grove.

In the park there was an odor like the odor of leaves burning, and it seemed impossible that anything could remain green after the heat of the day. Yet green was everywhere in the late sunlight, yellowgreen on the willow trees, blue-green on the tall Johnson grass and short clover, black-green on the shadowed trunks of the trees going up the bank to the playground where the dead grass was yellowgreen in the sunlight again.

At the playground a bunch of kids were fighting with their shirts off, wetting each other in the drinking fountain. When Blackie reached the top of the hill he saw Caleb helping a gang hold one boy over the stream of water with the boy's back down and his legs dangling into space on either side of the fountain. When he was loose the boy sprayed water over everyone, then helped the group catch another boy and hold him face down over the fountain, water pouring into his pants. The boys were all sizes and ages. Some were twice as big as others, and in a fight the little ones would have been mauled; but this was play. Caleb was dragging a bigger boy than he toward the fountain when he saw Blackie. He tried to cease playing and come over to his brother, but the big boy assumed the offensive and Caleb had to fight back. He fell on the ground and the bigger boy sat on his stomach. When he gave up at last the big boy let him free and he walked to the fountain of his own accord and leaned backwards into the stream of water washing the pebbles and dust from his grimy back. As he crossed to Blackie he grabbed his shirt from among the others lying on the bushes at the edge of the hill and, signaling for Blackie to help him, threw the other shirts into the limbs of the tree above. Blackie smiled and watched, but he did not enter into the play and when the boys began to climb after their shirts, shouting angrily as Caleb flipped them with his wet handkerchief, Blackie listened to the loud crack of wet cloth against bare flesh with a restless dissatisfaction.

A desire which he did not recognize, born when his cruelty to Mabel had freed him of the fear that she weakened and hindered him in his imitation of Whitey, made this childish cruelty seem beneath him. He felt that he was too mature for this. Though he had done the same thing in the spring he felt that he was a different and more important person now. He stood at the side of the field watching with the disdain of a man watching children until Crip came across the hill to him and the two of them walked down the bank from the playground toward the ballfield.

On the bank above the darkening ballfield they sat and played the guitar in turns, confiding to each other the tunes and words of songs, playing and singing. Gradually, by twos and threes, the boys from the playground came and sat about them until they were the center of a listening and admiring circle. Blackie sang in a falsetto, sweet and high, then Crip sang in a false bass, rich and low: snappy songs and nasal hillbilly ballads and sentimental dancetunes. Gradually, as it grew night, the boys in the circle went home, one by one, and at last Blackie was left with only Crip and Caleb and one other. Lying back with the soft grass and hard earth beneath his head, gazing up at the dark sky full of moist summer stars and smelling the fragrance of the park like the unnameable fragrance of the many plants in the country air

at night, he felt his restless desire increase without yet knowing what he desired.

Crip sang:

> *Roses of red are ready for plucking,*
> *Girls of sixteen are ready for highschool,*
> *Oh, don't do to me what you did to Marie,*
> *On Sat—sat—sat—turday night!*

When he ceased singing Crip told Blackie the names of
the stars.

—That's Venus and that's Orion and that's the Big Dip-
per which points to the North Star.

Blackie listened sentimentally to this information, the kind
that Whitey had sometimes volunteered when you did not
think he knew such things.

—What's the brightest star in the sky? he asked.

—Sirius, the dog star. But you can't see it now.

—How can it be the brightest star in the sky if you can't
see it? Blackie laughed.

—Because it don't rise until late at night, almost morning.
It's mostly in the sky in the daytime now.

—There ain't no stars in the daytime, Blackie said.

—Sure there are, only you can't see them because of the
sun.

—You're crapping me, Blackie said.

—Honest to God.

—If that's true think how much bigger than the stars the
sun must be.

—It's not bigger, it's just nearer, Crip explained. The

brightest star I was telling you about is one of the smallest, only it's the nearest to the earth.

Blackie laughed, uncertain whether or not Crip was kidding him.

—You've been crapping me, he insisted.

—No, I haven't, Crip protested. I've been reading.

Blackie thought this was very funny and wanted to grab Crip and roll down the hill with him wrestling in the grass. But you could not wrestle with a cripple, that was the trouble with Crip, and Blackie had always thought that he would rather be dead than deformed or maimed in any way. He wanted to die a violent death, to enter the other world as strong and great as he was in this. The idea of being sick or old and watching his body slowly lose all the attributes of which he was proud and waste away into a loathsome helplessness dependent upon others filled him with the same shuddering uneasiness as the idea of deformity. Laughing and shouting, he lunged at Caleb and the brothers rolled down the bank together leaving Crip and the other boy alone above them in the dark. At the bottom of the hill Blackie sat on Caleb's stomach tickling him and demanding until Caleb could not stand it any longer:

—Admit there ain't stars in the daytime! Admit!

—I admit, Blackie.

At ten o'clock they walked up the dark drive past the couples necking in parked cars toward the black angel of the peace monument and the entrance of the park. Crip and the tall boy attended them, one on either side of Blackie,

Crip telling more about the dog star, how it really was not one star but two revolving about each other, a heavy old star and a light young one, the connection between which scientists could not explain. Blackie listened inattentively, unable to believe in something that he could not see, and as he entered the shadow which the street lamp threw behind the stone pillar on one side of the drive he took out a cigarette. The tall boy, reaching across Crip to hand Blackie a match, brushed his arm against Crip's crutch. The crutch fell. Crip grabbed the tall boy, pulling him down into the dust and pebbles of the walk, and they rolled out of the shadow of the arch over the curb into the light of the street lamp, the crutch gleaming yellow beneath them against the black tar of the pavement, Crip shouting:

—You pushed me! You pushed me!

He was on top of the tall boy closing his fingers with all their strength about the boy's neck until his face was red and his eyes bulging out of their sockets, and all the time he was shouting:

—You pushed me! You pushed me!

Caleb bent over them and tried to pry Crip's fingers loose, but the crippled boy was too strong. Blackie stood on the curb holding the guitar in his hand and watching for a minute before he stepped forward and carefully kicked Crip in the side of the head with the heel of his shoe again and again until Crip released his hold on the tall boy's neck.

The boy scrambled up, his face scarlet and his eyes streaming. Crip let Caleb help him to his feet, then pushed Caleb

113

away and reached down for his crutch himself, almost falling again. Blackie stood between the two fighters watching them face each other, the tears streaming down their dirty cheeks and the breath wheezing in and out of their mouths in sucks and blows so violently that they were unable to speak.

—Who the hell do you think you're kicking? Crip finally gasped at Blackie.

—You could kill a guy like that, Blackie said.

—What did you choke me for? the tall boy sobbed.

—You pushed me, Crip gasped.

—I didn't push you, the boy sniffed.

—He didn't push you, I saw him, Caleb told Crip.

—I thought you pushed me, Crip gasped. I can't stand it when I think a guy pushes me.

—You ought to take it easy. You don't know how strong you are, Blackie said.

Crip did not look at Blackie or answer. The tall boy rubbed the tears from his cheeks with the back of his hand and felt his throat. Blackie watched him and Crip as they faced each other, the thread between solicitude and cruelty stretched to breaking in the intensity of his gaze, his breath almost as heavy as the breaths of the fighters.

—I didn't push you. I swear I didn't, the tall boy said, the tears suddenly silently overflowing his eyes again.

—All right. I'm sorry. I didn't mean to choke you, Crip said to him.

—You're both all right guys, Blackie told them laying his hands on their shoulders.

114

Crip jerked his shoulder away and turned on Blackie.

—Yeah! You ain't nobody to talk, he said. You didn't need to kick me in the head.

He crossed the street, swinging rapidly on his crutches. The others followed slowly and stood with him beneath the orange carstop sign waiting for the streetcar. No one spoke for a moment and in the silence their breaths were as audible as their footsteps had been crossing the street.

—Seen Dusty and Hatchet? Blackie asked.

—If I had I wouldn't tell you, Crip told him.

—He had to kick you to stop you, Caleb said.

—Yeah, Crip sniffed.

The trolley streaked toward them out of the dark around the curve of Piedmont Avenue. Halfway across the intersection it screeched to a standstill beneath the globe of the street lamp. Caleb ran and held the door until Crip reached it. The crippled boy boarded the streetcar by swinging both crutches under one arm and pulling himself up with the other. The tall boy wandered away up Thirteenth Street. The door of the trolley banged shut and the trolley streaked away down the curve of the street.

Holding his guitar in his hand Blackie stood beneath the carstop sign and watched until Caleb returned to the sidewalk and stood before him.

—I guess I'd better go home, Caleb said shyly.

He stood looking up at Blackie with quiet admiration. Blackie smiled at him bitterly.

—Come on, kid, he said. I'll walk you part way.

115

The job was endless but not fascinating. There was no climax or satisfaction. Until five o'clock it took his energy, but when he was off for the day there were still four hours of light during which he was restless and dissatisfied. There was nothing to do of enough interest to make him forget himself. That he did not go to see Mabel made him proud of his continence, but this single accomplishment was not enough to fill the time until the next day. He told himself that if he worked at something really interesting, like wrecking cars for the hell drivers, or if he drove an express truck always approaching a new city, it would be different. He would have given up his life gladly to any cause that enlisted him and demanded that he give his all. He was bored and he wanted excitement. But the evenings offered no cause. At five o'clock he walked to Pearl's house and bathed. There was seldom any supper there and he went to Mother's where it was ready at six. After seven there was only the park.

One evening he accompanied Albert to the YMCA where Albert showered and worked out each evening instead of going to his family's house on the outskirts of the city and returning to town after supper. The long moist concrete halls smelling of perspiration and lined on either side by rooms filled with boys reminded him of the wooden halls of the farm school. People passed like those he had mistaken for his old friends at the school the first day after his return when he was in the park. But he no longer imagined that he recognized them. He watched the young boys and the young office clerks exercising with ropes and pulleys and bar bells and felt for them only disdain. He had never exercised in his life—his favorite games had always been rock battles and chasing girls—yet he had the strength and body these people all desired and he could not be interested in their striving for a prize he had been given for no effort at all. He showered and swam and played tag in the basement pool where pale light fell first through a grating from the courtyard of the building and then through a frosted skylight onto the tile and clear water. But he remembered the country stream and the park and he did not return to the Y.

Another night the whiskeyeyed man with whom he worked gave him a ticket to a professional boxing match at Ponce de Leon Park, allowing him to wait until payday to pay. Blackie sat with the other workmen in the distant seats of the bleachers where cigar and cigarette smoke fouled his clothing and turned the air so blue and heavy that it was hard for him to breathe. But he liked this. The fight seemed to him an example of the way life should be, the action clearly determined, the goal known and capable of being obtained. The hunting instinct which never had been given enough open admission in the city for him to be aware that it guided and motivated his life, rose up in him in a great swell of images which he could not have put into words but which were clearly imprinted on his mind: the fighters, with the purple shadows of their embraces, the explosions of their back muscles, the pressure of their chests and of an arm thrown in backward curve about a neck, were like hunter and hunted, constantly metamorphosed, seeking each other through the smokeveined air which hung between them, a forest of transparent but solid crystal. Sometimes they seemed unable to find each other; others—they snapped together as though connected by rubber bands. But always the fight moved to its conclusion with the crowd roped off and excluded, the opponent met free from the confusing and weakening distractions of the world, yet within hearing of the world's roar of admiration.

On payday he paid the man for the ticket and, as Pearl was not home when he went to her house, walked to Mother's to eat. Caleb and Gladys were there, and after supper he led them across the street to the house behind the outdoor advertising sign where the old woman who occupied it had recently died.

The house was left as she had lived in it, locked up and waiting for her relatives to dispense with the furniture. Blackie picked the lock on the back door and, followed by his little brother and sister, crept into the silent house hot as an oven with all the windows closed and darkened by the signboard. With the brothers he had often gone shooting ducks in vacant houses, sometimes smoking the ducks as they found them, sometimes saving the tobacco. On tiptoes, he led the way through the rooms, shadowboxing now and then to the terror of his brother and sister, himself unafraid but striving to excite himself with fear. At the door to the bedroom he stopped. Gladys hissed in terror that she wanted to leave, but he shushed her and, passing through the doorway with Caleb holding onto his shirt tail, entered the room where the

118

old woman had died. The air of must and death still hung in the room. The old woman's cosmetics and clothes still littered the dresser and the open closet. And the fireplace was filled with discarded newspapers, letters, bills and medicine boxes. Blackie was suddenly aware of the presence of something important and awful. Stooping quietly he lit a match and held it to the rubbish in the grate. Flames leapt up in the midsummer heat. The shadows of their three figures and of the heavy furniture sprang into life, writhing and dancing on the walls behind them in the pink glare which reddened the room and faded as though a brilliant sunset were turning to night. Then Blackie shrieked:

—Open the door! Start the music!

The shriek echoed in the empty house followed immediately by the cries of his brother and sister and the crash of their feet and bodies as they ran for the door. Shadowboxing, Blackie ran after them, frightened yet proud of his sacrilege. In the yard he laughed at their fears and questions as to why he had shrieked, but he cautioned them not to tell Mother where they had been and, preserving the awe of the mystery, led them back across the street to the porch where Mother was seated surveying the street in the early August dusk.

—Come on and walk me to the corner and I'll buy us all an ice cream sundae, he said.

Mother accompanied them, complaining delicately that the heat chapped her thighs where they rubbed together and announcing that she was going to diet and lose weight. They ate four caramel walnut sundaes sitting at a table in the small drugstore, talking happily as they ate. But afterwards Blackie bade the others goodnight and, walking alone along the street in the firefly splattered dark, felt with dramatic satisfaction that he was less kin to them than to the writhing and dancing shadows he had seen on the walls of the empty house.

Sunday was blank. In the evening he went to the poolhall on North Avenue and played pool with the local boys who hung out there in the summer. For the first time he experienced the potency of a man of the world who has a roll of bills in his pocket. When he won a game he bought beers for himself and the fellows with whom he was playing, unfurling a bill from his roll, tossing it onto the counter and, after he had passed around the bottles, sweeping the change from the wet counter into the palm of his hand and dropping it into his pocket uncounted, as though it were nothing to him, merely a bribe to needful others.

The round billiard balls upon the soft green felt table and the talk about girls eventually brought his desire to see Mabel up into his thoughts and body, and when the game was over he said that he had an appointment and walked uptown alone. He told himself that he could take her or leave her now, but that there was no reason why he should not take her if he wanted to.

The uptown light at night was not white but colored, spilling red, blue, yellow, green and lavender onto the pavement. At a red neon sign he turned down the alley to the entrance and crossed the lobby to the staircase. But no one answered his knock on Mabel's door and he retraced his steps down and out of the hotel into the polychrome streets again.

In front of Miner and Carter's he met Albert and another fellow. They walked along together, meeting more friends on the steps in front of the library, and on Forsythe Street they entered a café and had a round of beers. Blackie talked to them with an exaggerated good humor and friendliness, relating stories of his conquests in which he included things he had done and things he had not done, appropriated out of stories he had heard from boys in the school and adopted to his own use.

When he saw the attention and admiration in their faces he drew his heel up on the seat of the booth, beneath one cheek of his buttock, with his pants leg rolled up and the muscles of his thigh tensed and expanded. Someone borrowed a straight pin from the waiter and Blackie gently drove it into his thigh just above the knee. He told them that it did not hurt. He could not feel it except for the initial prick because the muscles of his thigh were so thick that the pin did not reach through them. The attention and admiration increased. But Blackie felt too strong to remain in one place for long, with the boys in the warm beer booth, or beneath the crisscrossing wires and cables which roofed the curb at street corners. When they finished their beer and were on the street again he took leave of them as though he were going home and made his way back to the hotel.

Mabel still was not in her room, but as he was turning to leave a door opened down the hall and the redheaded friend of Mabel whom he had met once or twice came out of her room and said hello to him.

—She's not home, she said, but if you want to you can come in and wait.

He went into the girl's room, indifferent from the beer and yet aware that he could do with her what he wanted. The room was like Mabel's only more disordered. The Sunday paper lay scattered about the floor and a victrola sat on a table before the window with a dirty curtain ballooning in and out across it. The girl smiled at him and said something as she looked among the Sunday papers on the table until she found a record to put on the victrola. He sat on the bed making no reply at all, and when she came and sat on the bed beside him he kissed her once, without making any preliminaries, and pulled her back full length along the bed against him. She objected for a moment when the record ended, saying that she had to go turn off the victrola, then she came back and lay down beside him and said that she loved him.

The last light faded from the window while he was in the room. Before he left he heard Mabel enter her room down the hall, but he agreed with the redheaded girl, winking at her in a conspiracy he did not feel, not to tell Mabel that he had been there. He left the hotel and returned home still proud that he had not seen her.

For a week the sky continued cloudless and burning.

Then, on Saturday, in the shade at the side of the toolhouse when he received his pay envelope at noon, he announced to the foreman that he was quitting the job. The announcement was as much of a surprise to him as it was to the foreman. He was not conscious of having thought of it before, but as soon as the words were out of his mouth he knew that this was the right thing for him to do. All he made was money and the money made him no more able to pursue adventure as long as he was working. He was wasting his time being ordered around by a foreman. But things were going to be different now.

He returned to work with a wild elation. All of the joy of destruction welled up in him. He stood on the floor beams of a second story pulling out a windowframe and when he paused for the workmen below to lower the frame by ropes to the ground he picked up the weight from the window and threw it with a joy of sheer energy down through the plaster of the ceiling below. Dry plaster and lathing exploded about the iron bar as it fell, and when it struck the earth rose in waves of dust widening about him where he stood in the air, giving him such pleasure to watch that he momentarily regretted being free of the job. But a few minutes before five he climbed down from his place and on the stroke of the hour he bolted.

Walking about from room to room in her kimono, Pearl met him in the hall when he entered the house.

—There was a girl named Mabel here looking for you, she said.

123

Blackie felt capable of handling any new situation and answered her with the inattention of confidence in his voice.

—O.K. Thanks.

He went past her into the bathroom and ran his tub, but when he turned to come out she was leaning in the doorway watching him. He went up to her and pinched her cheek affectionately.

—She's a little old for you, isn't she? Pearl asked.

—Old enough.

In the bedroom he took off his clothes and returned to the hall wearing only his shorts.

—Look, Pearl said. I've been through all this. Don't get mixed up in something you can't handle.

He was surprised that she should compare herself to him, but not interested enough to want to talk about it.

—I can take care of myself.

—That's what we all think.

He stopped with his hand on the knob of the bathroom door and looked at her.

—I don't think it, I know it, he said giving her a smile as broad as a grin. So don't worry about it. She won't be coming around here any more.

—You're treating me like I was Mother, Pearl complained. I don't care if she comes around here. I just want you to take care of yourself.

—O.K., he said and closed the door.

He dressed in his black shirt. His hair was wet and black against his face which had sunburned on the job and peeled and sunburned through the peel until the cheeks were bright scales of pink beneath splotches of brown and dark orange. His neck was brown and freckled as it disappeared into the black shirt and his arms were freckled and brown as they came out of the sleeves, one wrist repeating the orange gold of his face with the gold of his bracelet. His teeth glowed as white as the towel with which he had dried himself, and against his dark chest a package of cigarettes stood out white in the breast pocket of his black shirt.

He kissed Pearl as he went out of the house and left her still standing in the hallway in her kimono.

On Spring Street he met Hatchet. Hatchet hesitated to speak but Blackie walked straight up to him, smiling, and asked for a match to light the cigarette he had stuck in the corner of his lips. Hatchet did not have a match, and Blackie told him to come on in a café with him and have a beer while he got some. It pleased him that Hatchet had hesitated to speak and it was with pleasure that he sat down in a booth opposite his old friend.

—You must be making a lot of money on your job, Hatchet said half impressed and half sarcastic.

Blackie waited until he had called to the waiter and ordered two beers before he answered.

—That job was crap, he said. I quit today.

—What are you doing now? Hatchet asked impressed.

—Oh, I've got something lined up. What about you?

The waiter brought two beers and a folder of matches. When he was gone Hatchet confided in a low voice that he and Dusty were almost ready to go through with their idea of stealing the bootlegger's car and asked if Blackie would be interested in going in with them now. Speaking in his normal tone Blackie replied that he was no more interested in the brothers' scheme now than before.

—If you're going to talk so loud about it I'd better just go, Hatchet objected.

He stood up in the booth and looked around to see who might be in the other booths along the wall to overhear them.

—Sit down, Blackie said jokingly, before I hit you over the head with this beer bottle.

—Yeah, and what would I be doing while you were hitting me over the head? Hatchet asked sitting down.

—What would you be doing? Blackie laughed. You wouldn't hit me over the head with a bottle would you?

—Sure, Hatchet sulked.

But he had decided to accept the conversation as a joke now that there was no danger of his plan being overheard and he smiled in accordance with Blackie's laughter.

—Here, Blackie said pushing one of the half-empty beer bottles across the table until it touched Hatchet's hand.

When he saw Hatchet's fingers fold about the neck of the bottle in burlesque defiance his anger rose as suddenly as his joy had risen in the afternoon. He swept the bottle out of Hatchet's hand and held it threateningly over him, spilling beer onto the table and Hatchet. He had not thought of threatening Hatchet until he was standing over him, but

126

now it was all he could do to restrain himself from smashing the bottle over the frightened boy's mole and freckle splattered head.

—Just touch that bottle, just touch it and I'll smash your skull right in!

He threw the bottle down onto the table, spraying the rest of the beer and foam across the wall of the booth. The bottle rolled from the table and broke on the tile floor with an explosion of shattering glass. But Blackie strode out of the café and up the street before anyone in the café realized what had happened.

A little beer had spilled on his pants and he stopped at a pressing parlor to have the Negro scrub out the beer and press the pants while he had his shoes shined.

Mabel was in her room at the hotel when he arrived. He entered breathing heavily enough for her to see that he was excited, and asked:

—Why did you come by my sister's looking for me today?

Mabel tried to be casual. Blackie was lighting a cigarette while he waited for her to answer, and she took one from the pack beside her on the bed and waited for him to light it also. Without comment, he held out the match. Mabel stood up just enough to lift herself from the bed, pulled daintily at her skirt, and sat down again before she leaned forward and touched the tip of her cigarette to the flame.

—Why shouldn't I come by your house looking for you? she asked. You come by here looking for me.

127

—That's right. And until I do you just stay here and wait for me.

—Oh, I guess you'd like that, Mabel said in a voice thin with tears. You haven't been to see me for over two weeks. What have you been doing, Blackie?

He could wait no longer to talk of the subject which interested him. He replied:

—I just frightened the hell out of Hatchet.

—Why did you do that? Mabel asked thinly.

—He thought he could get smart with me, but I picked up a beer bottle and frightened him half to death. I could have smashed his skull in just as easy as I could have touched him. You can bet he'll think twice before he starts anything with me again. Ain't that right, Honey?

—Why don't you think twice yourself sometimes? Mabel said.

Her hair was damp about her forehead and she patted the sweat from her forehead with a wadded handkerchief in an effort to show him, without going so far as to make him angry, that she was more interested in herself than in his fight. He had not sat down since he entered the room and still was standing against the wall opposite the bed looking down at her. Beneath her high forehead her cheeks and chin seemed tiny and pointed in the shadows of her eyes and mouth. Her dress was sleeveless and the vaccination scar on her sunburned arm shown white like the moon in the daytime.

Outside a radio blared the beginning of a night baseball game.

—I thought you didn't like him, Blackie told her raising his voice over the sound of the radio.

—I don't, but that's no reason for you to go trying to pick a fight with him, Mabel said. Why did you do it, Blackie?

—Look! He pretended like he'd hit me over the head with a beer bottle and I just showed him how tough it would be if he tried it. That's all. But he'll think twice before acting smart with me again or trying to tell me anything.

—That's no reason to try and start a fight, Mabel told him. I'll tell you that right now.

—He asked for it.

—After you made him, I bet.

—So what? He thought he could bluff me and I scared the hell out of him. Next time he'll know he's not as tough as I am.

—You knew that without threatening him.

—You don't like me for doing it, huh? Blackie demanded defiantly.

—I like you, but I don't see why you have to act mean to people the way you do, Mabel answered.

Blackie asked if she had a drink and, ignoring her answer in the negative, turned to the dresser and looked in one of the two small top drawers where Mabel sometimes kept a bottle. He wanted to be pleasant and happy with her as soon as he could find some excuse to do so without letting her think that he was giving in to her, and when he turned around, smiling as though he had just entered the room, he said:

—Let's go out and get a bottle.

—I bet you treat Hatchet just the way you treated me, said Mabel.

—Look! Let's drop it. I leave talking to women. You're good with words. O.K., you talk. But if you're going to talk to me don't think I'm just going to talk back. I ain't good with words. Talk to me and I'm going to do something. I'm going to beat the hell out of you, maybe, like Hatchet.

—And what happens when somebody beats the hell out of you?

Mabel stood up from the bed, and took her pocket-book, ready to go out. Blackie extinguished his cigarette in a pin tray on the dresser and put his arm around her waist.

—You wait until that happens to worry about it, huh?

His voice was tender and his hand rubbed her side.

—Oh, I'll wait, Mabel said. I'm used to waiting. I waited over two weeks for you to come to see me and you didn't.

—Well, I've come to see you now.

He kissed her and she kissed him back dramatically.

—Blackie, I don't like the world when I'm not with you, she said.

—I don't change no world for no woman, he answered pleased. Let's go get a bottle.

When they reached the door she stopped again and turned around in his arms.

—You didn't used to care about fighting and staying

away from me all the time. Now I don't think you care about me at all. You act like you're in a movie or something and I'm not even in the same room with you.

—Let's go get a bottle and come back, he said.

As they went down the stairs Mabel asked:

—Why didn't you come to see me earlier?

—Were you waiting for me earlier? asked Blackie.

—No, Mabel said.

They walked several blocks to an old residence on the edge of the business section which had a neon sign outside saying HOTEL. There were no rooms for rent but the people in the house sold bootlegged labeled whiskey. The man behind the desk took Blackie to the first room down the hall where another man produced a bottle of whiskey from a closet and showed it to Blackie for his approval. Blackie examined the unfamiliar *Mighty-Fine* label and said O.K., and after the man had put the bottle in a paper sack he strode out of the building with long self-conscious steps. Mabel was waiting for him on the sidewalk. Spitting into the gutter, he took her arm and started back toward her hotel. The shape of her figure under her tight dress made him think again with impatience what he had been missing for no reason at all and he ignored her suggestion that they go somewhere to eat or to the Boss Avenue Hall and dance. They would spend the evening in her room, he told her, the way she liked, playing cards and drinking and making love. Mabel acquiesced silently. In the alley from the street to the hotel he pushed her against the wall and kissed her.

—Whose girl are you? he asked.

—Yours.

—And what am I going to do to you when I get you back to your room?

—What?

Leaning against her he told her, content that they both wanted to do the same thing. Then he took her hand and led her inside the hotel and up the stairs. In the hall before her door he stopped. The door was open and the blond man from the Cuban Villa was standing at the dresser.

When he heard them the blond man turned and greeted Mabel. Mabel replied offhandedly and entered the room. But Blackie remained in the doorway suddenly covered with a fire of betrayal and anger. As though it had been obvious all along and he had been too stupid to see it, he saw that Mabel had not necessarily been waiting for him the two weeks he was working but might have been making love to the blond man every night. Even before that when he first knew Mabel and when he spent all his days with her the blond man might have been her lover. He had been right in staying away from her. She had used him and tricked him and now he was letting her trick him again. He threw the bottle of whiskey down on the bed, turned to leave, then thought bitterly that he had not bought the whiskey for Mabel to drink with someone else and turned to pick the bottle up again. As he did so, the blond man who had given Mabel a changepurse she had left the night before at the Cuban Villa passed him going toward the door as though that were all he had come for. But Blackie was not deceived by this. Grabbing the bottle of whiskey he shouted:

—Come on back and stay, you son of a bitch. I'm leaving.

He had reached the door to run after the man, but Mabel caught him by the back of the shirt.

—Wait a minute, Blackie, it's not what you think it is. Let me explain.

—Take your filthy hands off me, he snarled.

Shaking her as a dog shakes a tin can tied to its tail he lurched toward the door. Only her utter annihilation would satisfy him, only his escape from all consciousness of her existence. But she held onto his shirt and called his name, dogging him with her presence so he could not ignore it, until his shirt tail came out of his pants. Cursing her again he swung his fist around and smashed it into her face. The blow was so hard that it threw him off balance. Mabel let go of him and turned away spraying a crimson stream of blood across the clothes closet and wall.

—Here, Blackie said following her to the sink.

—Go away.

—Here, let me help you.

—Go away. I don't ever want to see you again.

—I'm sorry, but you shouldn't hold me when I tell you to let me go, Blackie said to her. You shouldn't ever hold me. I don't like it.

Bent over her where she stood at the sink he spoke in a low gentle voice trying to explain away his remorse. At the same time he felt a justified and predestined satisfaction in what he had done. The red blood from Mabel's nose fell into the white porcelain basin and drops from the running water splashed pink on the sides of the bowl. Blackie rested one hand solicitously on her shoulder and in the other held the towel. When her nose stopped bleeding Mabel took the towel and dried the water from her face with solicitous pats. Then she looked up into the mirror. The bridge of her nose was swollen to twice its size between her eyes and when she saw the reflection in the mirror she began to cry. Knowing the cause of her tears Blackie was not afraid of them. He patted her with both hands, his kindness increased by his growing awareness of deceiving her, and told her that he was sorry and that everything was going to be all right.

His thoughts as he bent over her were not of her but of her loneliness and separateness. He saw her not as she always had been but as an image romantic and alone, and he thought of her as he thought of himself.

Mabel let him kiss her as he led her to the bed and made her sit down. She had never known him to be so solicitous in his tenderness, almost feminine, and she looked at him a moment unbelieving. But he said:

—I love you.

And she replied with all her disbelief dispelled:

—I love you, too.

He smiled and kissed her gently on her swollen nose, aware of his kindness and cruelty as though they were things apart from himself.

—If you'd come to see me all the time, Mabel said, I

134

wouldn't go out even when you weren't here. I only went to the Cuban Villa last night because I hadn't seen you for two weeks and thought you might be there. After all, I did the first night, remember? I'd had lots of boyfriends before that, but I'd never been in love. Not even with my husband, though I thought I was. Even when I lived with him I didn't feel lonely when he was away the way I feel lonely when you aren't here. But it's going to be all right now, isn't it?

—Sure, he said and kissed her gently on the nose again.

—Don't. It hurts, she said.

—Some day I'm really going to hurt you, he told her with a passion born of his duplicity.

—No, you won't, Mabel said happily.

She snuggled back on the bed, pushing the pillow between her and the wall, settling comfortably and happily, her mouth pouted like a baby's with the desired taste of a sandwich and the bitter wash of beer already in it. As she smiled at Blackie sitting on the edge of the bed beside her she said as beguilingly as she could:

—Why don't you go out and get us a sandwich and some beer?

—Get dressed and we'll both go, Blackie said. I've got a date over at the Boss Avenue dance hall in half an hour.

Her red wet eyes looked at him in bewilderment from either side of her swollen nose. When she had walked back to the hotel with him he had told her that they were going to stay in all evening playing cards and making love the way she liked. The promise came back to her very clearly now.

135

—But I can't go out with my nose like this, Blackie. You said . . .

—I just remembered I promised to be there for a crap game. I can't go back on my gambler's word, can I, Honey? Come on and get dressed.

—Blackie, I can't go out like this. You'll just lose all your money if you go there . . .

—Not if I win.

The haze of evening was turning from blue to gray. In a flash of heat lightning a distant bunch of cumulus clouds lit up blue and white against the gray sky, then hung dully in the twilight like a pile of dirty bedclothes. Blackie walked out Marietta Street following the trolley line, not hesitating at street corners or traffic lights, and as the street neared the railroad and ran parallel to the tracks he took a shortcut across a vacant lot and along a path through weeds knee-high. He crossed a backyard lumberpile full of garbage cans and discarded automobile tires and entered the involved wreckage of dead automobiles not buried but strewn among the bodies of the living. A wire fence separated the used car lot from the greasestained foundation of the burned down service-station which was bordered by a desolation of Bermuda grass and lightning vine. He climbed over the wire fence and came out into the back street as it darkened and narrowed toward the dance hall.

The dance hall was hot and open to the night, but the toilet in which the crap game took place stank with urine and smoke and the accumulated heat of the summer. Sweat-

136

ing and inhaling the blue smoke which fouled the cloth of his shirt and grated his nostrils, Blackie rolled up his sleeves and fingered the bracelet on his wrist as he kneeled down waiting to enter the game. When it came his turn to play the dice rolled to a stop against the wall and he won as he had felt sure from the moment he entered that he was going to win. As he rolled a second time and won again a gust of fresh air blew through the room as someone entered and looking up he saw Crip.

—Hello, son, you sure get around, said Blackie rolling the dice and winning a third time.

—So do you, Crip answered. Come in the john with me, I've got something to tell you.

—Later, answered Blackie. I'm busy here.

In an hour the roll of bills in his hand had doubled and he was pleased and assured that he had known what he was doing when he quit his job. Mabel, he thought, would be impressed if she could see him now. Crip leaned against the wall among the crowd and waited. At last he made a bet with himself that if he lost twice in a row he would quit, and the second time he rolled the dice and did not win he stood up and announced that he was going to the toilet. Crip followed him and closed the door behind them.

—Too damned hot in here, Blackie said benevolently and opened the window which looked out onto the brick wall of a store back.

—Do you know that Dusty and Hatchet are out looking for you? Crip asked.

—No. Did they send you to tell me?

—I'm just as much your friend as I am theirs, Crip answered hotly. But it's nothing to me if they beat you up after you got smart with Hatchet this afternoon. I just thought I'd tell you.

—O.K., Blackie assured him confidently. O.K. I know you're my friend.

—I'm nobody's friend. I just thought I'd tell you.

Blackie bowed his head to him, smiling.

—I'm serious, Crip said.

—I'm serious, too, said Blackie. Come have a serious beer with me.

—No, I've got to go, Crip said putting his hand on the doorknob.

—Wait a minute, cautioned Blackie.

He raised himself up into the window and, while Crip waited, dropped down into the narrow passage between the brick back walls of the two buildings. Alone, he found his way out to the street. He was not sure where he wanted to go but he walked through the maze of streets up and down hills toward Lucky Street. In his pocket was forty dollars. But now he was thirsty and wanted a drink. Regretting that he had left the whiskey at Mabel's after all, he went into a café and ordered a beer. He downed the bottle at one tilt and walked out into the street again, full of satisfaction, swinging his short heavy body in long low strides from a center of gravity lower than his waist.

At the top of a hill he stopped. Behind him the glow of

neon reddened the sky. Before him the street dropped into darkness and rose again to another hilltop where the leaves of an oak tree were lighted by a street lamp. There were no cafés here, only houses, and one side of the street lamp was painted dark green to keep its rays from the already tree-darkened houses in whose windows no lights burned. He stood for a minute surveying the darkness, wondering if he had been wrong to leave Mabel and if he should go back to see her. Then he walked downhill away from the neon into the treeshaded blocks toward home where, strong and alone, the oak tree stood beneath the lamplight forcing its roots up through the concrete and over the stone curb, alone and strong against the city

CHAPTER 6

He could not sleep. The night was so hot that the occasional breeze only emphasized the heat. He sat in the window and played the guitar, hoping that Pearl would hear him and come talk to him, but instead she shouted for him to be quiet and go to sleep before he wakened Jeanette. So he put the guitar down on the floor and listened to the night noises: the rustle of leaves and creak of floorboards, the grind and roar of starting automobiles, and in the distance the barking of dogs.

That day he had seen a dog go mad in the street and the sight of the animal crazed and slobbering in the sunshine and the thought of himself as they said he would be if he were bitten, crazed as the dog and dying of thirst though even the sight of water would throw him into a horrible fit, had filled him with restlessness.

Everything he had done lately had seemed to go wrong. He did just what he wanted to do, yet somehow his actions seemed different when they were reflected in other people. He looked the way he wanted to in his own eyes, but Mother and Pearl and Caleb gave back a different impression from that which he had of himself. This made him angry, but his anger did not change their impressions. He knew that his idea of himself was the right one, that it was what he wanted to be. But the failing of others to see him as he saw himself angered him into suspecting that something of which he was unaware was wrong.

He had argued all week with Mother and Pearl over his quitting of his job. Both of them treated him as though this had been an act of weakness, and even when he insisted that all he did on the job was make money and that he could make more in crap games, they did not understand. Mother had said:

—You have to work to get what you want, Son.

—I've got what I want, he had answered.

Yet nobody understood that. Neither Mother nor Pearl nor Caleb nor Mabel understood him. Mother treated him as though he were a child who does not understand the seriousness of life, Pearl as though he were as emotional as she, Mabel as though she could make him do anything as long as she made love to him, and Caleb looked up to him with an admiration which, though at first he had enjoyed it, annoyed him now that he realized his little brother admired only the smoothness of his actions and not the strength and indifference which achieved them.

Sitting in the starlight, he fled in his mind from the conceptions which others reflected of him, and gradually, conditioned by his habit of labeling those people he chose to be his friends as good and those he rejected as bad, he decided that they must be bad in some way if they were against him. Dramatically, he told himself that it was necessary for him to choose between his ideal and these people who conflicted with it. He tried to think. He tried to be right. Mother and Pearl and Caleb and Mabel had all his affections and pleasures on their side, all the small familiarities which combat loneliness and make for happiness; but they also were contaminated by these things. Affection, happiness and pleasure were compensations of the weak. And his desire for an ideal strength, unpolluted by the compensations of the world, comfortless and even detailless, was so strong that the more renunciations were demanded the more strong it grew. Vague and vast as the night, his ideal appealed to him as the only recipient for the passion which it was necessary, to one or the other, for him to give. Yet all his feelings as he sat in the window wishing that he could sleep made him sentimental and increased the confusion in which, if he thought of these things, he thought that he must choose between them.

At last he went back to bed, hoping that he would go to sleep if he did not move for a minute. He lay perfectly still, his body heavy and dark against the white sheet, dark and heavy beneath his curved palm when he ran his hand down it. That was the way he should be to other people, unmistakable, the way his body was in bed. If only he could sleep. He longed for the oblivion of all consciousness, but he was unable to remove from his mind the pursued and pursuing images of himself. Just as sleep almost covered him, the images twitched him back to thought as taut muscles twitch a sleeper awake, and he lay in the bed rolling up the bracelet on his wrist until it cut into the flesh of his arm, then rolling it down again and feeling the intaglio bracelet imprinted in his skin.

Sidereal, his thoughts wandered backwards like a conversation among children seeking reasons for the conclusions with which they started. But he could find no satisfaction in thought comparable to the satisfaction of action; all thoughts seemed to him of equal importance, no one was separated from the others the way an action which has been done is separated from all other possible actions, and after a while they were all of equal unimportance.

Then he could think only to distract himself from thought, and thinking that he wanted a glass of water he rose to go to the bathroom and returned to sit in the window again and smoke a cigarette. In the southeast a bright star was rising. If he could go to sleep all the stars would be gone and it would be tomorrow in a moment. As soon as he closed his eyes, as though by magic, time would cease to exist. Yet as long as he thought, the same time passed slowly, minute by minute. The very idea tired him.

Leaning out of the window he watched the stars fade. It was almost dawn. Beyond the black filigree of leaves the sky was white with morning, and in the street below highway trucks were beginning to back in and out of the freight depot at the corner. He could hear the racing of motors, the impact of crates against loading platforms, the voices of starters and drivers; faintly he could distinguish the forms of blond wood against dark concrete, the fleshcolored faces and arms of the men against the drab silver of the trailers, and in his imagination see the drivers in the cabs high above distant highways where the sun came down clear and sharp at noon.

Sun filled the room. Pearl was shaking him and telling him that he must wake up. He pulled away and turned his face into the pillow to shut out the shape-destroying light from his eyes. But Pearl was shaking him and telling him that he must wake. With his eyes half open he ran his hand along the edge of the table beside the bed until he found a cigarette duck and stuck it between his dry lips. Then he felt along the table again until he found a folder with one match in it and lit the duck. The smoke drawn in between his lips made his mouth feel less dry, but he still could see nothing in the glare of sunlight and as he exhaled his swollen eyes crisscrossed back into oblivion.

Pearl was shaking him and telling him that he must wake up.

—Don't go back to sleep smoking or you'll set the house afire.

—I'm not going back to sleep.

—Well, then, keep your eyes open until I bring you a cup of coffee.

The words came to him slowly across the brightness and after the last word Pearl came bringing a cup of coffee. Stupidly, he sat up in the bed, the cup and saucer in his hands, the cigarette dangling between his lips.

—It's noon, Pearl said, and I want to talk to you before I go to work. Do you hear me?

—Why don't you let me sleep?

—Because you've slept enough. What's wrong, are you sick?

—No, I'm sleepy.

—Well, I've got to go to work and I want to talk with you.

Putting out the butt in the saucer he sipped the coffee and looked at her with a scowl. She stood in the sunlight at the side of the bed with a cup of coffee in her hands. Her face and body were in shadow but all about her streamed with brightness and the sunlight glinting in her hair reminded him of Mabel. She had wakened him from his sleep to start the chase again.

—Are you going to see Mother today? she demanded.

—Do you want me to?

He tried to sidestep the question and make whatever answer would let him escape from her the quickest.

—I want you to give her a message. She's seen Bob again and I want you to tell her for me that she's not to see him.

—Is that all you woke me up for?

146

—Is that all! shouted Pearl. Whenever anything happens to me all anybody can say is: Is that all? First Mother messes up my life by making me separate from Bob, then she sees him all the time. Everybody can see him but me. I'm just his wife. Well, I'm through. I thought you cared for me but I see you're just like the rest of this goddamned family, and I'm through.

Her shouting wakened Jeanette who began to cry in the next room and she ran out. Blackie knew that he should follow her and comfort her but he was too sleepy and half awake to get out of bed and he sat where he was looking after her. Besides, he was beginning to feel an enmity toward her hysterics as he felt toward Mabel's sentimentality. Perhaps no women deserved any respect.

Before she left Pearl came back into the room, patting around her eyes with a powder puff, and said that she was sorry. Her emotions had worked themselves out and she was calm. Pulling her face down to his lips, Blackie kissed her and said that he would go to see Mother: he still thought of himself as his sister's protector and of Mother as their comforter.

Saturday was cleaning day. Every piece of furniture in the front two rooms was pushed out of its usual place and in the kitchen Mother was on her hands and knees scrubbing the floor. Blackie stood in the doorway watching her and waiting for her to speak. She gave him a long look but returned silently to her work. She never worked hard except when she wanted sympathy, and when Pearl had re-

147

fused to return to Mother's after her baby was born Mother had pickled enough peach preserves to last a whole year. But Pearl had refused to return or enter into an open conflict with her and Mother had gone and stood on the sidewalk before Pearl's house shouting so the neighbors could hear that Pearl's baby was illegitimate because it had been born only six months after her marriage. At last Mother seemed to have a heart attack and Pearl came to stay with her for a while. Blackie had passed between them then carrying messages but now he was above it.

—What's wrong? he asked.

—What do you mean, what's wrong?

She continued scrubbing the floor and he remained in the doorway smiling at her. The dirty water and the rag with which she was scrubbing the floor filled the kitchen with an odor of damp earth. As she wrung out the rag over the pan of black water she gave him another long look, then she put her hand on the side of the sink and pulled herself up, sighing.

—I'm worried about Gladys and I'm worried about Pearl and I'm worried about money, that's what's wrong.

—Why don't you leave Pearl alone? he asked her. She can take care of herself.

He did not feel much patience with Mother but she amused him and he continued to smile.

—Oh, she can take care of herself, Mother said. Leave her alone one week and she'll be back living with that fiend. I'll leave her alone and let her take care of herself. Just like

148

I left that man who used to live next door to us alone after his wife accused me of trying to steal him from her because I used to help him up the steps when he came home drunk. As if I couldn't have stolen him from a hussy like her if I had wanted to. And he fell off the porch and broke his arm.

Blackie laughed.

—And what's wrong with Gladys?

—She's out all the time and I don't know where she is. She says she's practicing bowling, but nobody bowls ten hours a day, not in this weather, and she leaves after breakfast and doesn't come home until suppertime. So naturally she doesn't have time to help me about the house.

—Make her stay in, said Blackie.

—Just like I make you and Pearl do what I say? No, she's seen too much how everybody in this family does what they want to for me to be able to make her behave. But you could do something sometimes to help me with her it seems.

—Do you want me to make Gladys stay home?

—No, I want you to take her to a party. She's invited to a party next Saturday night by some girl who lives at the Hotel Edison but she hasn't got a date and I won't let her go alone. But I told her she could go if you would go with her.

—I'm not interested in going to any kids' party.

—Well, we can't always do just what we're interested in. Besides, you forget your sister's only a year younger than you are. Just come down to earth and act your age, Mr. Jobquitter. You're not a grandfather yet.

But she had ruffled Blackie's calm and he no longer felt like bantering with her.

—Maybe it'd make you happy if I got another job? he demanded.

—It certainly would not. School starts soon and you're going back to school. No child of mine is going to stop school to work.

—O.K. If it'll make you happy I'll take her to the party.

—Huh! Mother grunted.

To show that it meant nothing to her whether he took his sister to the party or not, she bent over, picked up the pan of black water from the floor and dumped it down the kitchen drain. Then she began to scrub the sink complaining as she worked that the house was a filthy place not fit to live in or she would rent out a room to make some money, and that unless the landlord agreed to paint the kitchen, which he absolutely refused to do, she was not going to pay the rent.

—I'll paint it for you, Blackie said with his humor returning.

—And where do you think I'm going to get the money to buy housepaint?

—I'll buy it.

—Oh, so you do have some money.

Her tone was full of sarcasm from the triumph of proving him a liar for he had said that he had no money when she had asked to borrow ten dollars the day he told her that he had quit his job. But she finished cleaning the sink humming to herself and told him to wait while she dressed to go to the store.

He accompanied her on the way to buy her Saturday groceries and they stopped first at a paint shop. Mother supervised the choice of color and examined each can of paint, demanding of the salesman a description of its qualities and replying to his descriptions with nodding squints of belief: ice blue for the kitchen and three small cans of red yellow and blue enamel for her lard cans and flowerpots.

Blackie paid for the paint, concealing the transaction from Mother whom he knew to have insufficient money to buy groceries for the weekend; then, while she went to the grocery store, he returned home alone to search in the garage for the paintbrush. The garage was a wooden shed which did not, since his father's death, contain a car, but which was used to store trunks and old furniture. The brush was lying on a rafter covered with dust. It took him a long time to find the brush and when he returned to the kitchen Mother was preparing dinner.

—Don't start painting until after we've eaten, Mother said.

Caleb was with her. She was making tomato sandwiches, red circles of tomato on white squares of bread, at one end of the table on which Caleb was stacking empty bottles from the shelves, and though she frowned at the bottles hemming her in she smiled at Blackie as she spoke.

—O.K. We need some turpentine to clean the brush anyway.

—Well, I'll send Cabie to the store to buy it. Take the change from my pocketbook in the livingroom, Cabie, and while you're at the store buy me a dill pickle and a box of saltines. Now hurry.

After they had eaten Mother stacked the dishes on the table and announced the order in which she wished the painting done.

—The back porch first, the kitchen next, and then the pantry. After that you can do all the lard cans with my ferns in them in the back yard. Now, the kitchen's all yours.

And she exited grandly fanning her face with the skirt of her dress.

Turpentine fumes rose in the heat, and as Blackie cleaned the brush his worries of the night rose from his brain and evaporated in the resinous fumes. He was sweating so by the time he began to paint that he removed his shirt and pants and worked in his underwear shorts which were soaked through with sweat and clinging to the mould of his short heavy loins. Nothing seemed to stand between him and his desire as he directed Caleb to help him carry the icebox in from the back porch to the kitchen and to cover the back porch floor with newspapers; and as he painted with the checkers of shadow and brightness falling through the lattice into his eyes he talked to Caleb as confidently as though talking to himself.

—Don't pay any attention to what Mother says, Kid, he told Caleb. You can't listen to women, I know. Mother and Pearl talk all the time and if you listen to them they'll mess you up. I almost let them mess me up but I caught on to things in time. All women do is talk and you can't answer them. They think they know everything but they don't know nothing and they can't do nothing and that's why they talk all the time. They think men are like them and that's why you have to be careful not to pay them much attention. If I listen to them I'd still be working at that sucker job now. And I'd be afraid to start out on my own. But I'm not afraid of nothing. I'm on my own and I haven't got nothing to do with what other people say. Other people only count when they're what you want and even then you've got to keep them in their place. Like when you get what you want from a girl the best thing to do is get up and leave her on the bed. The important things in a man's life he has to do alone, and he can't have women or nobody else telling him what to do. I've got lots of plans now about things that are important and I don't talk about them to nobody because I don't want other people putting in their two cents' worth. Maybe I'll tell you about them because maybe you'll understand some day, but I'm not telling Mother or Pearl and don't you tell them a word, understand Kid?

As he talked the thing he was going to do gradually became clear, passing before his eyes in the sunshine accompanied by the plash of the paintbrush against the wall and the mingling odors of turpentine and must from the melted ice. The escape for him to take became so obvious that he did not remember how he had been confused into thinking that he was hindered by other people. He did not have anything to do with others. He was alone; if there were any connection between him and Mother and Pearl and Mabel, he was opposed to them. He had mistaken them for his companions, but they were pursuers. The pettiness here was their pettiness and would disappear when he escaped from them. His fate was not here, and seeing it small he should have known that it was diminished by distance.

—You know that used car lot on Spring just above North Avenue? Well, there's a 1927 Ford there that I can get for forty dollars down payment and the rest when they catch me. And I've got forty dollars right here in my watch pocket. Don't mention it around Mother or she won't stop talking until she's got every cent of it out of me, but this afternoon I'm going up to that lot and take a good look at the motor and if it's not too bad I'll give the guy what he wants for a down payment and drive out of there. Maybe the motor ain't perfect but I can fix it so it'll run as smooth as new. And I'm going to give the body a new paint job. It's an ugly blue now, but I'm going to give it a coat of black paint that'll make it look so good even the guy who used to own it won't know it. That'll take all the money I've got, maybe, but money's not important. Oh, I guess it's important all right. Even people who like to do the talking listen when money talks. But getting it's not important once you know how. There's more where this came from. If you're the kind of guy who gets what he wants you don't have to worry about money the way people who try to save it worry. All they do is sit around and worry about where it's coming from. And if you do that you don't ever do anything else. But I'm the kind of guy who takes care of himself right away and wherever he is. Where I'm going trouble will be a matter of life and death. Anything less will be settled without talking. Nobody'll bother about little things like money. When I'm having a good time I'll drink and have a good time, and when I disagree with somebody we'll fight it out and the loser'll come and shake hands with me. I can find money without any trouble in a new town. Just like I can find a new girl. If I wanted I could ask Mabel to go with me and she would. She'll do anything I ask her. No kidding, she's that way about me. But I'm doing what I do alone. My motto is travel light.

He stopped to pick a paintbrush hair off the wall and Caleb asked him if he had seen Mabel lately.

—Not for a week. The last time I went by her hotel she grabbed hold of me when I was going out of the door and tried to stop me. That's the sort of thing women'll do thinking that you won't stop them just because they're women. But I let her have one right between the eyes and broke her nose. I didn't mean to but it was a good thing. You have to make certain things clear to women or they get too many ideas. Since then I've been steering clear of her, letting her think it over, but I've got me a new girl. She lives in a boarding house over near the Boss Avenue dance hall, both she and her mother in one room together. But they've got twin beds and when I stop by to see them I just crawl up on the bed with the daughter instead of sitting in a chair and the mother don't say a thing. And one day when Hazel, that's the daughter, wasn't there the mother said for me to come on in and stay a while anyway and I laid down on the bed with her. They all love it, don't kid yourself about that, Kid. They pretend not to so they can get promises out of you, but they love it. That sort of thing is important to them. But to a man the important things are something else.

He winked at his little brother, then paused and looked grave. There was only one paintbrush and Blackie was doing all the painting while Caleb watched and attended him and brought whatever he desired, a cigarette, a glass of water, turpentine to thin the paint as it thickened. Blackie was standing on the ladder painting the top section of the kitchen wall, straining up so the muscles in his bare thighs stood out in diamond shaped patterns like the diamond patches on a harlequin costume.

—Yes, he said, there ain't nobody of importance or nothing that counts in this town. I've gone as far as you can go here and I'm heading out tomorrow.

He lowered his voice, impressed by the importance of his decision, then ceased speaking. Mother was coming into the kitchen. She stopped in the pantry for a minute, then, shuddering and shaking her head, entered the room where they were painting and ran herself a glass of water at the faucet.

—Well, kids, it's beginning to look pretty good, she said. But be sure and get that place over the stove. I think you've missed a little place there.

156

Blackie did not answer, but when Mother had returned to the front of the house he descended a step of the ladder and leaned his face close to the face of his little brother and whispered:

—Slip in the pantry and bring me a little something!

Caleb smiled at him in embarrassment, not sure whether his command was meant seriously or not. But Blackie repeated it, descending another step of the ladder, putting out his cigarette so he could pantomime, and indicating the direction of the pantry with a jerk of his body and a click of his tongue as he swayed in the air.

—I'm drunk, he whispered. Paint fumes make you drunk. They all rise toward the ceiling where I've been working, and once you get drunk from paint fumes the only thing that'll sober you up is a little shot of whiskey.

The fatigue of the night momentarily returned to him as he stopped and watched his little brother slip across the kitchen toward the pantry. But the thought of his departure distracted him. Waiting, he wiped the beads of sweat from his forehead with his finger and flipped them toward the floor: the beads of sweat were cold and his forehead was hot. Then Caleb slipped back past the door from the front of the house and handed him Mother's mason ball jar of clear liquid. Blackie took a small sip, smacking his lips loudly, then another larger sip before he handed back the jar. The whiskey cleared his head and lightened his body and he fell into the rhythm of painting again heavily yet gracefully, like a heavy yet graceful animal leaping through the woods.

When the kitchen was finished they carried the ladder into the pantry and painted the small room. Silently and steadily Blackie worked, moving toward the finish of the job content in the knowledge that no one would find him here before he left. Toward all the people he knew he now had formed words which made it right for him not to see them again. He had worked out that each person was wrong, and to encounter one and find that he acted differently would only annoy him. Since he was leaving he was not interested in their little changes and differences.

This certainty, like the steady odor of the turpentine, dulled his senses, and when he heard Pearl and Mother talking in the front of the house a dull and senseless grin pulled the cigarette in the corner of his mouth halfway up his face. From between the deep darkness of his eyes and the separate hairs of a first beard which stood out now among the splattered round dots of ice blue paint on his chin, a half animal, an almost demonic expression leered. Mother's and Pearl's quiet voices grew nearer. Then they were in the doorway, come back to see how the work was progressing. Apparently their quarrel was over, but through the heat and fumes their presence reached Blackie as though through sleep.

—Oh, it looks simply wonderful, but it looks like hot work, Pearl said.

—Honey, you just don't know, Blackie told her.

Mother was determined to be congenial.

—Yeah, it turned out to be a real scorcher, she said. I'd

give anything in this world if we'd just have a good rain to cool things off.

—Oh, so would I, Pearl agreed vehemently with tears almost coming into her eyes. A real summer rain where everything turns black and it pours down for days and days so you can't even go out of the house but have to just stand in the window and watch it.

—Well, I don't think it needs go that far, Mother objected.

—Oh, yes you do, Pearl told her.

She was standing between Mother and Blackie who had sat on the ladder to rest while they were there and she put one arm around Blackie's waist and the other around Mother's neck, leaning toward Mother as though she were going to kiss her. But Mother pulled away and said that it was too hot for that kind of behavior.

—I bet you that it'll rain next week, Caleb said.

—Probably, Mother agreed. Dog days will be over then.

Blackie laughed.

—You don't believe in that stuff do you?

—Why not? Mother demanded.

—Look, Pearl said looking at her wristwatch and bringing their attention back to her. I've got to go in a minute. Come and walk me home, will you, Blackie?

She put as much appeal into her voice as she could, but Blackie answered impatiently.

—I've got to finish the pantry.

—Can't Caleb do it for you?

—Naw. But it won't take long if you want to hang around and I'll walk with you.

—I can't. I haven't got time.

Blackie had begun to work again and spoke without looking at her.

—O.K. I'll see you later.

—O.K., Pearl said.

The little of the pantry which remained seemed to take a long time to paint, but when it was finished Blackie told Caleb to clean the brush and straighten up the kitchen for him. Whistling, he washed his face and hands and pulled on his shirt and trousers watching the cloth turn dark as the sweat seeped through. A new surge of energy rushed through him as though a dam which had held it back was suddenly opened.

In the livingroom Mother was lying on the couch covered by a blanket and sewing on a new purple dress for herself.

—What have you got that blanket on for? he asked laughing and jerking the blanket away from her.

Angrily Mother grabbed at the blanket and held on.

—Leave that alone, she moaned whitefaced. I'm suddenly sick at my stomach. It must be that dill pickle I ate for dinner.

And while Blackie stood over her she belched a long exploding series of burps.

—What's that? Blackie laughed pointing at the mason ball jar half concealed between the cushions.

—That's the daily stimulant the doctor prescribed for

me. Blackie! where are you going? You promised to stay here until Gladys came.

—I'll be back, he called passing through the front door and across the porch.

From Mother's house, past Pearl's duplex, uptown to the used car lot, no pause interrupted his progress. He entered the gravel yard and walked across to the dealer's shed, and when he and the dealer reached the car he circled round and round it as though guarding from pretenders something which was already his. The dealer would not let him drive the car out of the lot for less than fifty dollars, however, and as he had only forty dollars he said that he would come back. He walked out of the used car lot and along the sidewalk with a set smile on his face so no one would see the determination in his heart. But he did not hesitate in choosing between his own fate and the unimportant fate of others. He had convinced himself that he needed the ten dollars and that gave him the excuse for anything he might do now to get it. Straight out Spring Street between plate glass windows, brick walls and the weeds and vines of vacant lots he walked until he reached the gravel yard of the Cuban Villa. Beside the round orange building a yellow Coca-Cola truck was parked to deliver soda and two men were leaning over the back of the truck talking like women over a fence. Passing them, he pushed open the screen door and entered the vacant afternoon interior. Behind the counter Crip's brother pushed the cash register drawer closed and looked up at him.

161

—Hello, Blackie said.

—Yeah? the man replied.

His voice was completely unyielding and unkind and it conveyed to Blackie all the assurance he sought. This man did not dissemble and would not hold a grudge; he did not give Blackie any encouragement and he would not have a store of resentment against him after he had spoken. He would not judge Blackie's words in the light of sentiment but of action for the silence between them was the silence between two men who are friends of necessity, Blackie told himself, and he spoke without hesitation or fear. He told the man that he was not a friend of Dusty and Hatchet and that he did not have anything to do with their plan to steal the bootlegger's car, but that he happened to know when and how they planned to steal it and that he was willing to give him the information. He needed ten dollars and the man could give that to him if he wanted to, or he could give him a job, driving a truck preferably as that was what he had done on the job he had just quit. All the time he was talking he was aware, as though he might have been watching the scene in a movie, that the man might turn on him any minute. But this made him feel no fear. It was simply a fact existing along with the fact of his decision and strength and determination. And when he finished and knew that Crip's brother and the blond man, who had come out of the door behind the counter and was standing beside the other, would have to do something, he waited with anxiety but with no fear.

162

Crip's brother looked at him silently for a moment, then told Blackie to follow him and went out through the door behind the counter. The blond man waited while Blackie came around the counter and went through the door into what he thought was a back room but which turned out to be the gravel yard shielded from the street on either side by tarpapered fences and open to the deadening sun, then followed behind him. When they were outside he grabbed Blackie from the rear and held him so tightly that his body pressed against Blackie's back. Facing him, Crip's brother frisked Blackie, feeling up and down his body until he found the knife which he had been carrying since he started gambling. Blackie gave his body unresistingly to the two men, trying to show that he belonged and understood and did not consider them his enemies.

—You won't need this, Crip's brother said pocketing the knife. And now listen to me.

Unresisting, Blackie listened. The flakes of isinglass on the tarpaper glittered in the sunlight fading the black of the tar and making him dizzy, but the words came to him clearly.

—I'm not giving you ten dollars or anything else, this time. But if you ever come back here again I'll give you something you're not looking for. I don't want no trouble from little pricks like you and those brothers and I'm not having any. I don't need you to double cross each other for me. This is a business I got here just like any other business, run to make money and not to give excitement to a bunch of stupid kids, and if you or any other kids are caught hanging around my garage, or around here even, I'll turn you over to the police who'll be just as glad to take you in for me as for any other citizen, and maybe more so. Now get out of here fast.

Blackie turned and went through the café, blinded by the sudden shadow so he had to feel his way around the counter and past the two men stacking crates of Coca-Cola in the corner, and out through the screen door into the sun and the crunch of gravel again.

Up Spring Street through the late afternoon sunlight and down Harris Street toward the cobblestone alley to the bus station he walked, a hard lump of anger in his chest drawing all his attention from the city about him. He was right and the bootleggers were wrong and he would do something to show them. He was not afraid of them. He was not afraid of even the ultimate violence. He was afraid only of doing something that would not make them sit up and take notice and see how wrong they were and be sorry that they had been wrong.

When he reached the end of the alley near the bus station he stopped in the shack of a Negro bootlegger and bought a drink to celebrate his determination. Jellybelly joked with him and called him Sir; he paid Jellybelly from his roll and walked gravely out into the alley again and up toward Baker.

A shaft of pink light like that from a house afire shot through the alley from the ball of sun poised on the horizon

164

of the housetops. Then the sun sank beneath the buildings, leaving the alley and sky colorless for a minute while its glow reappeared high above and spread a peacock's tail of red and gold across the blue feathered clouds.

Blackie was coming out of the alley into the next street. The block was deserted in both directions, and above the corner the street lamp, just lit, swung back and forth as though it had been struck. In the strip of grass between the sidewalk and the pavement a cricket chirped. Blackie walked down the driveway of cobblestones onto the pavement of the street, unaware of the empty dirty city about him as though he were the center of a universe which moved as he moved, pressing against him and stiffening his movements, but withholding all other universes from his orbit. Then he heard a rapid explosion of footsteps ack-acking across the concrete toward him from behind. In the twilight he swung around to meet them, but before he could recognize his pursuers a blinding red star exploded in his face. He fell. Legs revolved about him like the revolving trunks of trees. A fist swung, carrying the bright blade of a knife, and another descended with the heavy redness of a brick. He fought back with all the readyness held in his tense limbs, but the brick descended to his forehead and, as though falling a second time beneath the concrete, he fell from consciousness.

Time telescoped. When he came to he was lying on the cobblestones which led to the alley on the other side of the street. His mouth was full of blood and blood was running

165

down his forehead and leg. No one was in sight. He got to his feet, his head throbbing so heavily that he lost his balance, and fell forward onto the cobblestones again. On his hands and knees he crawled along the alley until he was standing upright. He did not feel any pain, even the throbbing in his head was only a weight, and he wondered how deep his wounds were beneath the blood on his forehead and leg. Drops of blood followed him up the alley, and when he careened into a garbage can the top fell off and clattered down the alley across the trail of blood behind him. The back windows of the houses lining the alley were lighted and Negro cooks were readying supper. But no one was disturbed enough by the noise to come out and see what had happened. He walked with no sense of time or movement, as painlessly as in sleep. On each side of him the dark wood of the alley fence passed and against it the enormous heads of sunflowers going to seed and bowed down by their own weight absorbed the last daylight into their yellow petals. He stumbled and his neck fell back with his mouth open staring up at the evening star. Then he leaned forward to spit and he was coming out of the alley into the block where Pearl lived. He cut across the front lawns, not able to reach the sidewalk, and mounted the long bare flight of stairs to the door. Inside he went to his room and fell across the bed, pulling the mattress halfway off, and lay halfway between the bed and the floor, clutching the mattress with both hands, cursing and crying.

He cursed his mother who had brought him into this
166

world, the city into which he had been born, the friends who had betrayed him by either encouragement or opposition, the strangers he had known—but most often he cursed them all at once:

—The bastards, the bastards, the bastards, the bastards, the bastards.

The tears streamed down his cheeks as he cursed aloud, hearing his words with a bitter satisfaction, sniffing at the end of each imprecation, and repeating his curses over and over until the torrent of obscenities comforted him.

When the wild reflex of hate was gone the physical pain began. He got to his feet, thinking that he might die from his wounds, and walked through the dark house. In the bathroom he reached up painfully and pulled the string to the light over the sink so he could see his face in the mirror.

What he saw made him begin to cry again. In the side of his forehead a soft dent was covered with hair and blood, his lips were swollen and raw, one ear burned with lacerations and his hair was red in several places from cuts in his scalp. Gently, weeping and letting the salt tears roll over his cheeks and burn his raw lips, he took off his clothes and examined his body. Parts of him of which he never before had been aware ached with concentrated awareness. There was a knife wound so high in his thigh that his assailants must have aimed higher; his body was covered with black and green bruises, curved like teeth marks on a body that has been bitten, where he had been kicked with the heels of shoes; and something had happened to one of his fingers.

167

Nothing was visible on the finger, but it hurt more than any of his other wounds, as though the center of the bone had been bruised. Gently, he wet the washrag and tried to wash the cinders and grime out of the torn flesh of his lips and forehead and thigh, but the most gentle touch of the cloth was unbearable. Crying and wanting someone to help him, he dropped the cloth onto the floor and wandered through the house calling Pearl and turning on the lights.

There was no answer.

A housecoat hung among empty hangers in the open clothes-closet. Empty cosmetic jars lay open in the drawers and on top of the dresser. The frame of the baby's bed was bare, the bedclothes and mattress gone. Without comprehending Blackie walked into the bare hall calling Pearl's name. She was not in the kitchen or on the back porch. In his bedroom on the floor he found a folded sheet of paper with his name on it which he must have knocked from the pillow when he fell across the bed.

> Honey—I thought you would be here before I left and I could talk with you. But it's almost time for my bus and I have to go. I left Jeanette with Bob's family in the country this morning instead of going to work like I said I was. I am going to Jacksonville Florida to stay and I will send you my address when I know what it is. I want you to tell Mother for me as I don't want to hear her rave and am not telling her. The rent is paid here for the rest of the month so you can stay. Then take the furniture to Mother's or if she don't want it sell it and keep the money for yourself. I

know you understand me Honey, and I think I understand you and love you most of anybody in the world but I can't stay in one place any longer, anyway not this city.

                                        Love, Pearl.

It was night. Going to the kitchen he poured himself a glass of milk and tried to drink it, but his swollen lips could not bear the touch of the glass and the milk ran over his mouth and down his chin onto his naked body. When he saw the drops of white milk on his dark flesh, everything else ceased to matter. A wave of pity for his torn and bruised body swept over him. His body seemed the only thing in this world which was real and was his. He touched it gently, weeping for it, so innocent and so wronged. How could he have allowed such a thing to happen to it? He should have wanted nothing from this world except someone who loved him and attended his body and comforted him. Why had he allowed himself to become helpless and alone? He would give all the greatness and ideals he had ever striven for if someone, Mabel or Pearl or Mother or Gladys—or even Caleb—would come to him now and comfort and care for his bruised and torn flesh, so unjustly pained and maimed, and he wept for himself gently and from the bottom of his heart.

Then he remembered the money.

As rapidly as he could he limped to the bathroom and picked up his trousers from the wad of clothing on the floor. His fingers felt the bills, squarefolded and heavy, through the cloth before they could draw them out. Then he had the money in his hands and was counting it. The forty dollars was all there. A snarl of pleasure rasped through his sobs and bloated his tearstained face into a smile. All his growing love and pity were metamorphosed instantly into bitterness and pride. He had triumphed over them after all. The bastards had thought they had gotten the best of him by attacking in a group and from behind. But he still had everything and he had triumphed over them. He had what he wanted and he was free of the whole caboodle as he had never been free before.

His hate and pride mingled in a joy wilder than his remorse had been. He began to laugh hysterically, standing naked in the bathroom, and then to cry, mingling sobs with his laughter. With what righteous and grateful and proud satisfaction he would revenge himself upon everyone now, leading them a chase through places they could not follow for he had often followed with them and knew where they turned back afraid. With what pleasure he would pulverize their flesh or snap their bones as easily as he would tear a sheet of paper or snap a match between his fingers. At the very thought a tenseness of satisfaction reached a climax and exploded in his muscles and bones. Smiling and sniffing, he strode out of the bathroom and through the house, turning out the lights as he went, the money clutched in his hand, the flop of his bare feet across the floor and the sniff of his laughter the only sounds in the dark.

He did not wonder who his assailants were. It did not

matter. Violence had freed him from everyone. Individuals were not important, and he would revenge himself upon the whole world. There was no one whom he did not hate and from whom his heart could receive sympathy; and as he lay his bruised face gently against the cool sheet, his heart went out in dry sobs not to the memory of Whitey, whom he had forgotten, but to the memory of Whitey's loneliness and the contempt with which that loneliness had turned away from the suffocations of sympathy to stern and final forgetfulness.

CHAPTER 7

He had several violent dreams.

He was standing in front of a prison wall when convicts broke in long wavering lines running slowly toward him ducking and zigzagging through the open field, and another guard gave him a gun and told him to use it, shooting to wound but not to kill. But the prisoners were already running past him; he was in the middle of a wide flat field with a few men far apart running past him and he began to aim carefully and shoot for their eyes or the sides of their foreheads and when one came close he rammed his bayonet into him to stop him and stamped into his face with his heel as he lay in the dust screaming and screaming.

Then he was safe in bed though there was a rat in the covers somewhere, or rather he was not in the bed but lying on the floor in the bedcovers and there was a rat in the blanket moving visibly beneath the tubes and tunnels of the cloth as he sat up watching and advancing his hand

173

beneath the covers, brushing his arm against the rough wool of the blanket, watching the concealed shape and hoping to catch it about the neck, crooking his fingers to grasp when the rat buried its row of myriad white teeth into his wrist. He jerked his arm out and the rat came with it, dangling in the air, holding on by its teeth, and his blood curling oil like into the saliva in the rim of its mouth until he beat hammered pounded and smashed the skull in with his fist as an alarm began to ring.

It was the phone. He stood up, his mouth dry, his eyes unfocused, and flopped topheavily down the hall. It was Pearl and she said she had been trying to get him everywhere. He did not make any very coherent answers but he agreed to everything that Pearl said when she told him that she had been talking to Bob and that she was leaving town the next morning to go to the country to see his folks for a week and that she wanted Blackie to stay at her house with the baby while she arranged everything. He did not remember finishing the conversation but he had gone to the bathroom and drunk a glass full of warmish water and started back to the bed, but he turned out of the hall into West Peachtree Street and was driving backwards guiding in the little round concave mirror on the windshield when the bright idea occurred to him to see if he could follow the lines of neon reflected in the black pavement past the sign saying Used Cars that he saw clearly in red and black letters, dark boarding houses, secret private hospitals, when he ran tail on into a black sedan going fast. He was tight

174

but not drunk and he saw the man and woman with their pink looking flesh like the rich have standing looking at their c-r-u-m-p-l-e-d, crumpled, fender and he reached toward his back pocket as he stood on the trolley track gleaming silver where the tar of the street was all rose and black and he swayed in all directions as though his feet were nailed to the street while he took a card out of his wallet to give the man. He was tight but not drunk and with the card balanced on his palm he wrote the curve of the first letter of his name which suspendedly began to blacken itself in slow motion across the white of the card but though he tried to hurry he could not for it was the dream in which he was pursued on a tricycle up a steep hill and could not could not could not . . .

He pushed all the covers off him. It was the middle of the night. He wished he could sleep until morning. He had once in Mabel's bed, but now he got up and stood by the window, or no, it was the dresser for it was in the slanted mirror that he first discovered that the lower part of his stomach where the hairs curled down to his pubes and his pubes and thighs were clotted with grit and covered with dry blood. He stood a minute in horror examining the sore skin and then he heard *her* coming up the stairs and down the hall and quickly he turned out the light and slipped nude into the bed and pulled the covers up to his chin pretending to be asleep. But he listened as she turned the key in the lock and turned the knob and turned on the small lamp beside the bed and when she leaned over in the dimness and tried to slip her hand under the covers he caught her wrist. He was breathing evenly, still pretending to be asleep with his eyes closed, but he caught her wrist and held it. She wiggled her hand hotly and said that she wanted to touch him there, just once. He said no, and she asked why? He told her but she did not believe him. Then he said yes and throwing back the covers turned to watch her face when she saw. But when he saw her she already had turned translucent and as he watched she turned transparent and vanished.

This frightened him and he fled. He was fleeing through water for there was water everywhere and the car he was trying to reach was on the highway under the watercolor-washed sky disappearing in the white unfinished corner of the day with water swirling about in the storm and mixing the colors like the colors on the sheen of oil in a gutter, red orange yellow brown purple blue . . . and when he had almost reached the white concrete (or was it the base of the stairs) a motorcycle crashed up the steps with an ear-splitting screech of brakes and a crash that shattered the wooden banisters into fragments. A child was hurt. With a swoosh and bang the ceiling fell in the hall behind him and in the damp plaster smell and the light shafted fog of the upper hall people began to run about. Moooootttttthhhhher. A child was hurt somewhere. He tried to fight his way up pushing aside the caved in sections of the wall and ceiling and wreckage of the banisters, but he never could get the car out of the mud. Sunlight shafted through the dust. Flowers were blooming. He had a drink. And he was calling

176

Mabel where are you and the child was still calling mooooo-
ttttther.

He did not remember any of this.

One foot thrust from beneath the sheet, one hand hanging in space over the edge of the bed, he awoke. It took him
a while to know where he was and what had happened the
night before. From the window light myriad and granular
pressed like anger against his eyes, and closing his eyes he
lay motionless and listened to the sounds about the house.
The light was raw and glaring and he could not tell the
hour, but there were footsteps of several people walking on
the floor below and he knew that it must be late. He did
not care. Almost a week had passed since his assault, but
each morning the resistance to consciousness and the anger
grew.

The first day when he awaked in Pearl's disordered and
half empty house he had been filled with the necessity of
doing something at once, and he had known that he did not
want to see anyone or speak to anyone. He had dressed and
left the house without even looking at his wounds in the
mirror: they were not yet proud scars but were still signs
of weakness like the disfigurations of disease and age which,
if he looked at them, would betray him to himself in a bit
less surety of walk as he entered a room where Mother
or Pearl or Mabel were and knew that they would pity him,
or in the expression of his eyes as he looked at the brothers
or the men at the Cuban Villa and wondered, as though he
were a weak woman and could only wonder about such
things, if they were his assailants.

He left the house and rode the streetcar, his eyes cast down to the corrugated floor between the straw seats so he would not see anyone he knew, to the end of the line near the Federal Penitentiary. There he caught a ride with a salesman in a new car out the Macon highway. When he got in the car the man looked frightened of him, but Blackie did not give a damn what the man thought, he was going to hitchhike down one coast of Florida and up the other. The ride carried him to south Georgia. The hills flattened as he went, the plowed fields gave way to grass and groomsage burned brown and orange by the dog day heat, and the grass and broomsage in turn gave way to stretches of pine trees sparse of needles and blacktrunked as though they had been consumed in a forest fire. The earth was the color of dried blood. He was nearly to Florida. But when the salesman stopped for the night in a small town he did not hitch for another ride. Instead he walked along the dirt road out of the turpentine town brooding over the thoughts which had formed in his mind during the afternoon. And fear was added. And from fear a sense of shame. And from shame, anger. He was afraid that the sons of bitches would think that he had run out of town because he was afraid. Somehow they had tricked him into doing exactly the wrong thing.

Brooding, he walked out the dirt road hoping that he would reach another town where there would be no one who knew him, not even the man who had given him a ride. But after half an hour of walking through the dust and resin odor

178

accumulated by the long yellow heat of the afternoon, he was still in the midst of a flat uninhabited stretch of pine trees. He realized that it might be hours before he reached another town, and in sudden and complete reversal he turned and retraced his steps through the unbroken dusk, alternately feeling pleased with the idea that he would return to the city and show the sons of bitches who was afraid, and miserable with the realization that he was not back in the city yet, that he was in the forlorn midst of nowhere. His muscles ached with the anxiety of what he imagined was happening in the city in this wasted time. He could see the blond man at the Cuban Villa and Crip's brother with his whiteskinned beardstubbled face laughing, nudging each other and winking, and the brothers in the center of a circle beneath the swings at the playground telling all the guys and girls from the lake what had happened, and the black bastards at Jellybelly's strutting with self-importance when there were no white men there and laughing:

—Yeah, that little old white kid that use to come in here drinking licker like he was a man got the tar beat out of him right up the alley there and left town lickety-split, hahaha, lickety-split . . .

When he reached the square of the town he crossed the highway, pretending not to notice the men who were watching him from beneath the tin roofs over the sidewalk of the stores, and entered the lunch stand which was open at the end of the railroad station. He sat at the counter and ordered a plate of ham and eggs, a cup of coffee.

179

A group of boys hanging around in the corner by the door were arguing about the standing of the Crackers in the Southern League the year before.

—I bet you ten dollars they was in first place.

—You ain't got ten dollars.

—I bet you ten dollars I got ten dollars.

—Ha ha ha ha . . .

Listening, he thought how stupid they were, and sneering to himself he glanced at them from beneath his lowered eyelids as though hate and observation were the same thing. He pretended not to be aware of their existence; but just let one of them notice him or say something to him about his wounds and he would show them just as he would show everybody else in the world.

He felt the opposite of the way he had felt the day he was returning from the school. Then he had been almost afraid to see anything outside himself for fear that it would make him cry. Now he defied anything to touch him. As he ate he tried to will one of the boys into making a move toward him, and he hated not only them but the man behind the counter and the station attendant who passed the door back and forth across the screened rectangle of darkening sky. He had been a fool to think that the world would be any different away from the city. The whole world was the same, the whole world.

He had almost finished eating when a train came whistling and chugging into the station. He stopped, his knife and fork poised in the air, and demanded of the man behind the counter how long the train stopped there.

—Don't stop unless there's a signal out for it. Just slows down.

He hesitated until he saw the last car passing the station, then dropped his knife and fork onto the plate before him and ran for the door. Sprinting as fast as he could along the cinders and crossties, he ran after the train until he caught the handle at the side steps of the last car and boarded it just as the train was swinging into the flat bank of grass which curved out of the town.

The coach was empty except for the conductor sitting on a seat at the front end. When Blackie entered he looked up with annoyance, came and collected his fare, and returned to the seat at the end of the car where he remained for the rest of the trip sorting through a bunch of dirty papers in a strongbox on his knees.

Blackie sat in the middle of the coach and stared at the window where dark descending on the landscape outside drew the green from the pine trees and the red from the earth until the window was opaque and reflected the dirty interior of the coach, green mohair and red enamel lighted by round yellow ceiling globes, and he stared at his own reflection stiff and stark in the glass.

Beneath the viaducts through the city the train came into the station. Full of defiance he climbed the long stairs from the tracks to the entrance and the wide paved square which led over the bridgelike curve of Spring Street viaduct, above the city's dry river of cinders, smoke and steel, to the gleaming reflections of neon in the downtown trolley tracks.

But though his eyes searched as much now, upon his return, as they had cowered and hidden upon his departure, he saw no one he knew. Violence seemed to have isolated him. As he passed through the colored and steaming night streets, through slowwalking crowds of people, watching every face, it was as though he were in a strange city where every person was a stranger, and though he passed the café on Forsythe Street and all the theaters on Peachtree, he did not see anyone he knew. When it was late he climbed the long steps and slept at Pearl's house in the same disordered and half empty room which he had left.

In the morning he went to see Mother, carrying Pearl's note with him. But first, while he was dressing, he looked at his wounds in the bathroom mirror. Of those on his head the purple splotches about his mouth and eyes had faded, the cuts in his scalp closed, and only the hole in the side of his forehead remained open and ugly. The bruises on his body did not worry him for they could not be seen when he was dressed, and the wound on his thigh was healing. Only his finger, on which there was nothing visible, still hurt; but pushing his hair forward so it hung over his forehead he told himself that he could forget the finger if he wanted to.

Mother was seated in the living room, a pair of spectacles balanced on the end of her nose, and trying to thread a needle so she could continue sewing on the dress which Gladys was to wear to the party. He walked up to her, held out the note without saying anything, and hoped that she would not notice that he had been in a fight. She took the piece of paper with annoyance, thinking it was nothing of importance and not wanting to be interrupted, but when she read it she became wild. She did not notice him or his wounds. She began to shout that someone had to stop Pearl before she did something to ruin all their lives, and she did not listen when he told her that it was two days since Pearl had left. She did not even realize that he had been out of town, and her complete ignorance of him angered him as much as her harping on what had happened to him would have angered him. He left the house without saying anything more to her and without answering her calls to him to get ready to go after his sister.

He went uptown and bought himself a new suit. The day was ordinary, not like the night before had been. He ran into some people he knew, and though his rebuff of them was not as violent as it would have been earlier, he dismissed them all with the same sneering and insolent remark, and waited for the dark hardening of his wounds into scars.

Opening his eyes he saw his little brother standing at the foot of the bed in the eye squinting glare.

—Mother says you can't have any breakfast if you don't get up now.

—I don't want any. How about bringing me a glass of milk and running me a bath, huh, Kid?

His return had been the day before yesterday. Last night he had taken his little sister to the party. Now he was lying awake in the back room at Mother's. Beyond the window-frame in the raw light he could see the garage, and on the

183

other side of the bed when he turned his head away from the glare, the heavy carved dresser, too large for the room, Mother's clothes and cosmetics, kept here even though she slept up front with Gladys when he was home.

—Here's your milk.

Drinking the milk he almost returned to sleep and imagined that he was already in the tub with the water booming down over him when Caleb's voice, speaking again, brought into perspective the booming of the water in the tub at the far end of the hall.

—Gee, do you know what happened last night? Mother read it in the paper, on the front page, when I brought it in to read the funnies. Dusty and Hatchet were in a wreck on dead man's curve. They'd tried to steal a car and those bootleggers who run the Cuban Villa were chasing them and ran into them right there on Peachtree Road. It says one car was full of whiskey and there was whiskey everywhere all over the street. And Dusty and Hatchet are in the hospital but it says they aren't seriously hurt and tomorrow they're going to be taken to the City Jail where the bootleggers are.

The crackle of the newspaper close to him grated on his ear.

—Here it is right here. Do you want to read it?

—Naw, Kid, you told me. I'm going to take my bath.

Frowning he got out of bed and with his eyes nearly closed walked across the room. As far as he was concerned Dusty and Hatchet had asked for what they had got. And only an

184

empty nausea had risen in him at the image of shattered glass on black concrete smelling of whiskey.

Putting his hand on the doorframe he turned into the hall. Caleb followed him.

—Had you heard about it last night, Blackie?

—Naw. But it don't surprise me. Leave me alone, Kid. I've got a hangover.

The tub was full, clear, white and hot. His body sank into the water like a rock sinking into a clear sea and sloshed a tidal wave over the back of the tub onto the bathroom floor. The slosh echoed in the bathroom, silent except for the drip drip drip of the water from the tub and the tick tick tick of the clock lying on its side above the sink. Empty and guilty, as though he were being pursued for some crime which he could not remember, he soaked in the hot tub listening to the drip of the water and the tick of the clock. Yet he did not feel either guilty or empty for what had happened to the bootleggers and the brothers. He was glad of that. But the emptiness was immense, as though his feet sticking out of the water beneath the metal faucet were mountains rising from the waters of a distant sea, and the guilt covered him as though his body were fouled by a tiny parasite which could be neither seen nor removed.

The remembering of who and where he was had left him with a feeling as though he had been another person and now was accused of what that person had done. He felt that before he had slept he had drunk and acted too much and had given away or lost something which was not his to lose

185

or give away. What it was he could not quite remember. Yet the memory pursued his consciousness like a word on the tip of his tongue which he could neither say nor forget.

Standing up he soaped himself, impatiently rubbing the white suds all over his dark body; then he submerged himself in the water again, washing off all the soap. But the feeling of emptiness and guilt remained, and pitting effort against effort he tried to remember in detail the events of the night.

While he was away the wisteria vine over the garage in the backyard had come out in a second blossoming brought on by the long heat of the summer; at seven o'clock the night sky had been almost dark and, silhouetted against the darkening sky over the garage, the wisteria vine had distorted the shape of the building, its thin purple clusters washed of all but their last tint by the fading light, their dry fragrance filling the air with a simultaneity of autumn and spring.

As he stood at the bedroom window in his underwear shorts, his shoes and socks, dressing for the party, the scent of the wisteria from the backyard drifted into the room and reminded him of the landscape of pouring April rain through which he had ridden to the farm school in the beginning of summer: drenched in rain whole orchards of peach trees had mounted and descended the hills their black branches veiled in mists of pink blossoms and green buds; pink water had filled his footprints as he walked across the oozing mud of the school yard in the sudden sunshine, and from one side of the dormitory the buzz of bees and the sweet bathpowder odor of wisteria had come to him from the purple blossoms heavy on the leafless vine.

Turning away from the window he turned away from the memory and stood before the mirror buttoning his black shirt. The pearl buttons of the shirt were white, white thread stitched the seams around the shoulders and down the button flap in front; and when he had buttoned the shirt he took and tied his white silk tie, weaving his dark heavy hands over and under each other and watching them in the mirror until he pushed the small white knot into place. Then he raised his eyes and looked at the reflection of his face. Just beneath the hairline on the right side of his forehead a scab was half formed over the bruised circle of flesh where he had been hit with the brick, but no visible sign of his other wounds remained. Pushing his hair forward over his forehead he turned to pick up his pants.

—Do you know who hit you, Blackie?

—A friend of mine.

—Gee, did you report him to the police?

—It's my head and my friend and nobody's brick so it's no business of the police.

Dismissing the subject as he had dismissed it before in the afternoon, he took his pants from the bed and curtly told his little brother to hold them for him while he put them on.

Caleb fumbled with the pants awkwardly.

—How?

187

—Here!

Impatiently, standing in his shoes and socks, shorts and shirt, he showed his little brother how: the cuffs of the trousers were to be held one in each hand by Caleb while Blackie, facing him, held the waist in his hands and slipped a leg through a leg of the trousers. When it could go no further Caleb would drop the cuff and the trouser leg would slip on without touching the floor.

—All right, Caleb said. I understand.

But when he held the trousers he did not let go of the second cuff in time and Blackie's leg caught in the trousers and scuffed the cuff against the dusty floor. A curved smudge of dust discolored the dark cloth and Caleb leaned to brush it off.

Blackie, annoyed with the attention, said:

—O.K. You'll learn in time.

The distress in his brother's movements annoyed him. Admiring no one he did not like to be reminded so closely of admiration; and after he had put on his doublebreasted coat and folded a handkerchief for the breast pocket so all the corners pointed up, he descended the stairs. In the living room Mother, dressed in her corset and stockings held up by corset garters, was pinning a corsage of sweetpeas on the shoulder of Gladys' dress while Gladys watched in the mantel mirror.

—Hold still if you want me to get this done, Mother muttered between lips clenched over a mouthful of pins.

—All right, but hurry, Mama.

—All right, you're all ready now.

—No I'm not, I've got to get my stuff upstairs.

His feeling for them was not even of annoyance, only of waiting, and he suffered Gladys to kiss him and say he was the sweetest brother in the world as she ran past him and up the stairs. Mother did not acknowledge his presence for a minute but patted her hair with her fingers as her eyes swept past the mirror and she turned to pick up her purple dress from the back of a chair.

—Now take care of your sister and act like a man tonight, Son, she said at last.

—I am a man, he replied following her into the hall. Can you lend me five dollars?

Mother looked him up and down.

—Certainly not. Women never lend money to men.

He did not need the money, but he knew that some precaution was necessary since Mother had seen his new suit to keep her from trying to borrow money from him. He had asked her first so she could not ask him, and he was pleased with himself as he stood in the lower hall with Caleb waiting for Gladys to come down.

—You'll be in high school and I'll be in junior high this year.

—That's right.

Gladys clattered toward them on high heels and grabbed Blackie's arm. Caleb followed as far as the porch and called a last greeting as they turned up the sidewalk.

—Goodnight.

—'Night.

His feeling of waiting, the gulf between what he sought and what he found, colored the whole party. The party took place on the third floor of the Edison Hotel where the girl who gave it lived in a room with her mother. She kissed Gladys and said hello to Blackie; then the girls disappeared into the apartment and Blackie went across the hall into the large unfurnished room where the dancing was to take place. The room was bare except for a wooden chair on which a victrola sat. A group of boys and girls stood about the chair changing records as the victrola ground out music. The only person dancing, however, was an old harridan in the middle of the room at whom everybody else looked. She was alone, whirling about with one hand to her bosom and the other straight out from her shoulder. Dipping and swaying she circled the floor, and every now and then, smiling wildly, caught at the skirt of one of the young girls who lined the wall and flipped it into the air. The boys and girls giggled and whispered and shouted. Blackie, at the far end of the room from the door, stood with one foot on the sill of the window and waited.

To this ordinary crowd he had nothing to say. Boys and girls crowded into the room now and started dancing. Some that he knew came and spoke to him, but he did not hear what they said or answer them. Like a man in a foreign country the language of which he does not understand he impressed them with his mere presence. The impression he strove to make was not the same he had made in the dance hall earlier in the dog days, but cruder beneath the despotism of distance and waiting.

—Come on and dance with me!

Gladys was hissing into his face.

—Naw.

—You've got to, you brought me. Just this first dance. I can take care of myself after that.

Leading her backward into the forest of dancers he saw Mabel and a man he did not know come in the door from the hall and after them Dusty and Hatchet. A thrill of expectation went through him. This was not at all the kind of kid party he had thought it would be and he was about to ask Gladys how the hell she got mixed up in a crowd like this when the record ended and she whispered thanks and was gone. One second she was there and the next she was gone, so he returned to the far end of the room and stood with one foot on the sill of the window and waited.

He could see Mabel passing in and out of his view among the dancers and he knew that she had seen him. Once he caught her looking in his direction, but she turned her eyes quickly away. He waited for the end of the record, knowing she would come to him then. The brothers could wait, or they could come to him too. He was not going to them. Then the record had ended and another started and he saw Mabel talking to the man at the other end of the room. Angrily, he realized that she was not going to come and speak to him. But she had another think coming if she thought he would come to her. He stood and watched her,

191

a whole conversation with her passing silently through his angry thoughts. First she came up and asked him the reason he had not been to see her. He replied that there was no reason, that it made no difference to him whether he saw her or not. Then she said that she was afraid he blamed her for his having gotten hurt and he replied that no one she knew was capable of hurting him. Next she tried to play on his sympathy and said that she was so lonely sometimes without him that she thought of killing herself. This made him really angry and he twisted her arm up behind her, as he had done once before to keep her from leaving him, and told her that she did not know the meaning of the word lonely, that if she did she really would kill herself, but that she couldn't be lonely if she had to as long as there was anybody left in this town for her to sleep with.

He stood with one foot on the sill of the window. He was through with her. He would not even speak to her if she came to him. But he had to release his anger in movement and he pushed his way through the crowd to look for the brothers. He passed directly back of Mabel as he went toward the door and he jostled her with his elbow, staring at the man with her and hoping she would send the man after him. But the man did not follow.

He looked over the whole floor of the hotel for the brothers and finally asked a boy if he had seen them. The boy replied that they had left right after they first came in, and Blackie returned to the large room where everyone was dancing. Mabel saw him as he entered, but as he passed she

192

turned frightenedly away, pretending not to have seen him, and he passed by, ignoring her now but still staring at the man.

Standing at the window with one foot on the sill he looked down toward the street. He had insulted Mabel and she had taken it and he was through with her now. On the sidewalk a group of boys in purple sweaters were entering the hotel: Fred Dendy, Frank Jefferson, Shorty Smith, T. J. Donaldson and Red Warren. Turning, he watched the door until the boys entered the room and began searching through the crowd. They found him and they suggested the game, but he led the way back to the hall, moving stiffly and importantly through the crowd.

In the bathroom he allowed the circle to form about him while he knelt on the floor contemptuously shaking the dice in his fist. Then he took off his coat, loosened his tie, and looked slowly around the circle of stupid eager faces.

Suddenly a knock came on the door and a woman's angry voice ordered them out of the bathroom. Wiping his forehead with his handkerchief he led them out into the hall. He felt the heat as he had not felt it all summer and a steady throbbing had started in his temples. Waiting, he wished that he were in the park pool swimming out to the far raft, dipping down beneath the warm surface of the lake to the cool depths which would scrape the heat from him as sharply as a knife, or lying on the boardwalk, cooled by the water, his body as dark as the body of the lifeguard drifting in the rowboat in the aftersupper breeze.

193

Someone cautioned:

—Stick together. We'll find another place.

He was standing in the doorway to the room where the boys and girls were dancing, when Gladys came up to him and asked him to dance with her.

—Once was enough.

—Come on, she hissed at him. I've got something to tell you.

And as he put his arm about her waist and backed her onto the dance floor she whispered rapidly into his ear:

—It's so hot here a bunch of us are going down to Eunice's house. Don't say anything and pretend like you're just going downstairs for a minute. But meet me, do you hear?

He left her in the middle of the record and returned to the hall to tell the rest of the boys who had been in the crap game that he had a place for them to go. When they were downstairs he needed a drink and with one of the boys he went around the corner to a bootlegger's. They each bought a bottle. When they returned Gladys and some of the others had gone, but she had left a boy with a car to show them the way.

In a 1927 Ford they drove down West Peachtree to a gray frame house and walked up the three flights of steps which ascended the steep bank of the front yard from sidewalk to porch. Gladys was waiting for him seated just inside the door in the front room that was full of tapestries on the walls, whatnots and ornaments in all the corners. She jumped up when he entered and popped a piece of divinity fudge into his mouth. He ate the candy looking around the room. This was a real kid party, the girls all sitting, the boys all standing around, and with a nod to one of the guys from the crap game he started down the hall for an investigation.

The game started again in the bathroom. It was a large room, lighted as the first had been by a bare bulb on the ceiling which cast the shadows of the boys onto the floor like the shadows of trees on hard clay beneath the midday sun. But it was bigger. There was enough room between the tub and the toilet with a watercloset on the wall above it for them all to kneel in a comfortable circle.

Then, when the game had started a fat loud woman opened the door and shouted:

—There'll be no crap games in the bathroom at this house. If you want to shoot craps go into the kitchen and leave this room for what it's for.

The game began a third time in the kitchen. Kneeling in the large room Blackie took a long swig from his bottle of whiskey and passed it around. In the circle of boys whiskey gave him the kind of assurance sleep once had given him when he was alone, but even in the center of the kitchen with the windows and the doors open the heat made his body sweat and his consciousness center on himself. He felt his underwear wet around his waist and his new pants, tight in the crotch, cutting him as he knelt; but the wetness and tightness took his attention from the throbbing in his head and he pulled at his trousers with pleasure. Whenever he won he took another drink to celebrate, and when he lost he took a drink to pass the time until the dice were his again. Between throws he was alone. The people in the game did not exist, only the two white cubes with black dots on them. It was against their strength that he pitted his strength. Caressing the dice he spoke to them softly, begging them to be good to him or cursing them for the harm they had done. Time after time they rolled across the patterned linoleum and increased or decreased the pile of money at his feet. They too, he felt, knew the tenseness of strength within begging for release without involvement among others, they too relaxed with the whiskey, and they too saw only him, watching his two brown eyes with their forty-two black ones.

But something foreign, some memory which had been trying to come up with the sickening feeling that accompanied his waking each morning, also took advantage of the divinity fudge and whiskey. An uneasiness, like the feeling of approaching nausea, took hold of him.

He was sick. Rising to his feet he left the dice in the bright heat of the kitchen and, walking as slowly as though he were walking through warm water, made his way up the hall to the bathroom. The hall seemed like a passing freight train and it took him an interminable time to reach the door. When he entered the room and switched on the light, he fell back against the closed door and shut his eyes. But for a moment he had seen the sickeningly bright orange sun and clay of the lightglobe and walls.

He was on the sunbaked earth between the first and second dormitory, almost halfway where the chinaberry tree casts the small single pool of shade. Leaning against the hot metal of a parked automobile he was watching the fat-assed boy and the sneering superintendent of the school walk across the bright clay toward him. The night before the boy had touched Whitey's guitar where it hung upon a nail in the dormitory wall, and Blackie had leapt from the top bunk onto the boy's back and beat his head against the floor until a crowd of other boys came and dragged him off. In the heat of the morning he knew that at last the boy had reported him to the superintendent.

As they met the sneer on the superintendent's face widened into an open snarl.

—I know what you're after, his voice boomed in the bathroom, and if you're not careful you're going to get it. But it won't do you any good. So you may just as well stop causing trouble around here and get out to that goddamned field and go to work. I'm going to keep you two apart from now on and maybe you'll learn who's in charge around here. You got by with being liked and playing high and mighty as long as you could. But he's in trouble now, and you'll be in trouble too if you don't get the lead out of your ass. But you'll not be in the same goddamned dormitory together.

Cringing with all his might Blackie tried not to hear more, not to allow the explosion to enter his memory. But the shot of the gun rang out, echoing in the bathroom as it had echoed in the country.

A barbed wire fence ran along the clay from the first

dormitory to the chinaberry tree and from the chinaberry tree to the second. Blackie ran alongside the barbed wire fence as fast as he could toward the second dormitory. The building was two stories high, and above the second story a barred oval window opened into the hotbox of a punishment room where solitary sentences were sweated out. The sun, directly overhead, outlined the entire structure with sharp midday shadows before the wavering fields of heat; and the sound of the gun, exploding like a flashbulb in his eyes, imprinted every detail of the scene before him in a negative and bloodred haze. He knew the gun. A friend had smuggled it to Whitey one visitor's day, and Whitey had buried it in a cigarbox beneath the streamside oak tree where they swam planning to shoot tin cans off the far bank when they could get some ammunition.

Boys poured out of the dormitory door like blood out of a wound. Blackie fought his way through them and into the building. On the stairs he stumbled and fell to his hands and knees, running on all fours until he was upright again, but he did not stop until he reached the top of the stairway. Someone was there before him. The door was open. A barstriped oval of light was reflected in the dark pool of blood which was widening about Whitey's head.

Lunging forward without moving his feet he caught the bathroom wall and vomited into the toilet bowl.

Down the stairs from the second dormitory, across the yard to the first, and up the stairs to his bunk, he walked speaking to no one. Boys came and tried to say some words

198

of comfort, but he refused to look at them or to answer. He refused to believe that they could feel or understand what he felt. Finally, they left him alone. He lay in his bunk, afternoon and night, until morning, and just as the sun rose he rose from the bunk, awake and fully clothed, and left the dormitory. No one spoke to him or tried to stop him. Down the steps past the monitors into the sun, up the dirt road from the school to the highway, and along the stretch of grass between the highway and the pine trees, he walked carrying the guitar until he caught a ride.

Retching, he pushed himself upright, lost his balance and retreated in a series of rapid backward steps into the door. Then he pulled himself up, holding onto the side of the tub, and stood before the sink.

The memory of the fear he had felt for what he had seen in the mirror above the old fashioned sink brought back the fear as terrible as before and with it brought back what he had seen: his face burned out by the sun—beneath each eye a dry riverbed, between the riverbeds a bone gnawed clean by dogs and bleached by heat, below the bones a crack in the baked earth flecked with the scum of an evaporated swamp. He had blinked and rolled his eyes but the dead eyes in the mirror had remained motionless. Turning on the water he had lowered his face to the sink and washed the vomit from his lips, but when he raised his face and looked into the mirror he had seen again the same Gargaphian image. He had drawn back his fist and struck the glass. The glass had crunched. Drawing back his fist a second time,

199

he had struck again. The glass had shattered and tinkled splinters white and silver over the basin and floor. Where the mirror had been a square of blank dead cardboard had remained.

In a dilution of the terror he had felt the night before, he stood up in the tub and leaned forward, water dripping from his body to the floor, so he could see his face in the mirror above the sink. He half expected to see the apparition of the night, but his own face appeared. It was worse for dissipation, dark circles beneath the eyes, the features heavier and coarser beneath the skin, and the expression hard and set; but it was his face, dark and handsome as it was each morning when he examined it in the mirror, and all his wounds were gone except the scar on the side of his forehead.

Stern and final forgetfulness! He laughed at his weakness of guilt and memory. He had been guilty of the weakness of remembering and of not putting his strength into impressive action. Now, he knew not to remember. He knew not to think, only to act, and now he would do something which would show his strength clearly and impressively to one and all, something right and perfect.

He did not want to remember more, he was through with the past, but as he sank into the mealy water the end of the memories which he had already loosed flowed over his mind.

Fleeing from the shattered glass on white tile smelling of vomit, and from the heat of the bathroom, he had walked up the wooden floored hall in the opposite direction from

200

the crap game in the kitchen. His temples had been throbbing so that his head had seemed to expand each time the blood had pulsed through it and he had wanted fresh air.

Faintly, thinly, tricklingly, he remembered walking onto the porch where a girl had stood leaning against the banisters. Who she had been or what she had looked like he did not remember. But she had spoken to him and grabbed his arm as he passed her, and he had struck at her and gone on descending the steps from the porch to the yard without pausing. With his feet in the air just above the surface of the concrete, he had descended the steps from the yard to the sidewalk until he fell. He had risen to his feet effortlessly. In the chiaroscuro of the midnight street the acromatic light had ranged downward through a scale of grays to black. Above him in the house had been bright voices, and a dying voice, an older identity, had bade him return and have fun for himself; but its call had been no more than a cry, not an animal sound perhaps, but not a word to be listened to and obeyed. Instead, a passion of greed for what he had that they did not have had overcome him. He had laughed at the idea of letting go of his sufficiency for anything which he might get from them. All that he had needed had been a few more drinks, one at the bootlegger's where he had been earlier, one at North Side, one at Jellybelly's.

He dried on a woman odored towel and with the towel wrapped around him padded on bare feet to the bedroom. Caleb was waiting for him.

—Why didn't you wake me when you came in last night?

201

he asked. We were here in the same room all night but I was asleep and didn't know it.

Blackie did not want to listen to anyone.

—Well, maybe we'll go out tonight, Kid. We can have a double date. I know a girl who'll be just right for you. O.K.?

—Sure, Blackie.

—O.K. I'll come by the place where you stay for you about suppertime.

Yes, he was through with memory. It was necessary, he told himself dogmatically, if he were to give himself to action, not to think beforehand what his actions were going to be, not even if they were things which he had done before, and not to remember what the results of those actions had been, not even if he deliberately had to conceal the known results from himself.

Dressed in the clothes he had worn the night before, he descended the stairs. In the hall he met Mother returning from the front door, a triumph of outraged confirmation in her bearing.

—Well, what do you think of this? she demanded. A special delivery postcard, *postcard* mind you, from Pearl in Philadelphia, Pennsylvania. Only a child of mine could start for Jacksonville, Florida and send you a card from Philadelphia, Pennsylvania.

Indignantly, she handed the card to Blackie and marched toward the kitchen. Blackie stood in the hall holding the postcard, a picture of an unreal hotel bathed in a light no day ever possessed and surrounded by none of the confusing and distracting details of a city. But he did not turn the card over and read the message.

Gladys slipped by on her way from the living room to the porch.

—Honey! she whispered gliding past him in the hall. Don't tell Mother you didn't bring me home last night. All right?

The screen door banged. Blackie turned and entered the livingroom, looking about it like a man looking about a room for an object which has been hidden on his own person. He put the postcard behind the column at the end of the mantel and took down the photograph album. The livingroom was empty, but through the window he could see Gladys on the front porch and from the kitchen he could hear Mother's movements. Impassively, turning through the pages of the album one by one, he tore out all the photographs of himself. When he came to the last page he placed the album once more behind the column at the end of the mantel and stood in front of the fireplace ripping into bits the photographs in his hands. The bits he threw into the grate. Then he walked through the dining room to the kitchen. Mother looked up at him from the table where she was shelling peas into a pan and stuffing the pods into a paper sack, but she did not speak and he returned through the back porch and up the bare hall to the front door.

—Hey, look across the street, Gladys giggled in a stage whisper. There's a man walking down the street in a white

203

suit. It's the doggone funniest thing I ever saw in my life.

He did not heed her but walked across the porch, letting the screen door bang behind him, and up the street through the raw glare of the afternoon. The day was overcast but the raw sun hurt his eyes. Trees and buildings were faded and insolated. The field of Bermuda grass which he crossed at the corner was white and slippery beneath his shoes, bleached by the sun of all lifecontaining green and filling the air with a dry odor like the odor of hay. He turned into North Avenue, a parade of trucks passing him up the wide street, their bodies disfigured by lettering and covered with frayed tarpaulins, their brakes grinding and their chains clanking over the intersection. Beneath the cover of their noise he thought that he heard someone call his name. He stopped and looked in both directions, up and down the street; but he saw no one, and as soon as the trucks were past there was no sound, only the echo of silence.

At West Peachtree he turned away from the traffic toward midtown. He had come back and settled his accounts with people, yet he felt only tenseness and expectation. He felt that there was something, perhaps the only thing he should have done, still left undone; but he did not know what it was. He could do anything he wanted to. Nothing restrained him or bound him. The strength of his body was heavy and self-exciting. He had only to decide that he should do this or that, and he could do either of any two opposite things with equal ease. But no restraining fragment of the yearning he once had felt held onto his thinning and tensening identity

204

to oppose it and give it direction; and nothing outside him seemed to indicate what he was to do.

He passed deserted Sunday buildings of cream and red brick, vacant lots where outdoor advertising signs of dark green enclosed words against which his mind neither struggled nor stayed, the vinecovered dark stone and wood of decayed houses, the plate glass windows and tile floor of an automobile showroom, a parked car etched in the sun, smelling of hot metal and reflecting the curved streets and buildings in the chromium headlights, up hill and down, and finally a field of burning grass billowing thick black clouds of smoke into the sky.

Then, at the bottom of a hill he stopped and rubbed his hands across his loins in staglike satisfaction. Looking up he saw the pale circle of the daytime moon, that dead planet which gives light, and beyond the city over East Point and College Park, dark clouds which no wind would blow away but which would descend slowly and steadily in rain. But it was something else which had stopped him. Retracing his steps to the top of the hill behind, he stood on the corner. The ventilator of a dry cleaning plant droned steadily. Turning, he walked to the middle of the block and sat down on the curb, his back to an oak tree in a vacant field which overlooked midtown, his face to a block of identical brick houses. With his knees wide apart and his elbows resting on them he smoked a cigarette and stared at the houses, and when he had finished the cigarette he flipped the butt into the gutter and crossed the street to a house with the name of a photographer engraved in gold letters on the glass door. He stopped for a moment at the foot of the stoop, adjusting his body, then mounted the brick ironrailed steps and rang the bell.

He was smiling and pleased with himself. All the uneasiness with which he had awakened was gone. The spot on the side of his forehead was a scar now, old enough to be remembered without pain and no more noticeable than the white starpatterned scars on his sunburned hands.

He had decided that no one was home and was turning, ready to leave, when the photographer came up the hall and opened the door. The fact that he had nearly gone made Blackie feel that the meeting was fateful.

The photographer wore a leather apron, his shirt sleeves were rolled up and his brownstained fingers were wet. With a recognizing smile full of large yellow teeth he greeted Blackie by name and asked him to come in and wait in the room at the side of the hall while he finished putting some negatives in fixer.

—I'm O.K. here, Blackie said.

The wall was lined with photographs of expensively dressed women sitting on upholstered benches in front of artificial backgrounds. Looking at the pictures, he waited. And as though without reason Whitey came into his mind. But there was no longer any mystery in Whitey for him. With the pale disillusion of discovery he realized that he knew, perhaps had known for a long time if he just had thought of it, why Whitey had killed himself. There had been no reason for Whitey to return to the school or to have stayed away, and that was why he had come back, to show them that they were not important enough for him to stay away. And that was why he had shot himself, to show that he had more power than they did and that he was concerned with himself alone.

The photographer returned and, finding Blackie still in the hall, pointed out to him a photograph of Dusty and Hatchet which hung upon the wall among the pictures of women. The photograph was in the same soft focus as the others and did not look much like the brothers to him; besides, he was no longer interested in the brothers. He was no longer interested even in Whitey.

—How do you like it? the photographer asked.

—It looks lots better than they do.

—Oh, that's because I've removed all their freckles and moles, the photographer said. I try to make pictures look as much like people as possible, but in a way that looks best. I hope you'll let me take a picture of you before that suntan fades. You'll look terrific with the suntan and in a white shirt instead of a black one.

Blackie frowned.

—I don't allow any pictures to be taken of me.

—For heaven's sake why?

—No reason, I just don't like it.

He looked at the photographer closely and with disdain: the photographer's etiolated skin was so white and covered with black hairs where it came out of his shirt at the neck and sleeves that he looked as though he had never been in the sun. But he would be agreeable to the photographer unless the photographer annoyed him, unless he touched him; but if the photographer touched him he would let him have it.

—Well, the photographer said and Blackie noticed that his breath was heavy with whiskey, come on back in the kitchen while I mix us a drink.

He followed down the hall and through a dark middle room into the kitchen.

—What's yours? the photographer asked.

—I don't know. I've got a sort of hangover.

—In that case what you need is a hair of the dog.

The photographer poured shots in two tumblers and handed one to Blackie.

—Do you want a chaser?

—Hell, no, Blackie grinned. I ain't the kind of guy to build a fire and then piss on it.

The photographer laughed with him and he was heavy with self-pleasure again.

He downed his drink. Then the photographer poured two more and with his glass in one hand and the quart whiskey bottle in the other led the way up the hall to the front room. Blackie watched him and waited for something to happen. He did not pay any attention to the dark room, painted black and lighted by a red light, which the photographer showed him. He was thinking that perhaps this was what his return to the city was building up to, that something important was going to happen. The photographer had sat on one of two yellow loveseats which faced each other across a low glass table and invited Blackie to sit down, but he remained by the door conscious of his importance. There was no reason for him to have come to see the photographer and he ought to get something for it. Killing time, he examined all the objects in the whitepainted closetlike retouching booth in the corner of the room while the photographer watched him over the back of the loveseat. He barely noticed the brushes and inks and pencils as he pushed them aside to look at the pane of ground glass with a light beneath it. Then he opened the drawer beneath the shelf. Scattered among the papers and appointment pads were the uninteresting contents of the photographer's pockets, coins and keys and pills, but far in the back was a small pearlhandled revolver. He wanted it instinctively from the moment he saw it, but he closed the drawer and came out of the booth without saying anything.

The photographer again asked him to sit down, but he hesitated halfway between the retouching booth and the loveseat and looked unseeingly at the contents of the cases along the back wall. If he had known what he knew now, he was thinking, there would have been no reason for him to have returned to the city. It did not matter any longer where or when he did anything, for he could do anything any place and any time. So if he wanted the gun he might as well take it so that there would be some point in his having come to the photographer's. And suddenly he wanted the photographer to touch him, just to touch him and give him an excuse for anything he might do.

—Seen Dusty and Hatchet lately? he asked.

—Not for a couple of weeks. I guess they're up to something. There are a couple of boys who aren't afraid of life.

Blackie wanted to bring attention to himself, not to the brothers, and he changed the subject.

—What are these, victrola records?

He was standing beside a case of square black albums.

—Yes. Play them if you want to. You can always do whatever you like in this house, you know, just like Dusty and Hatchet. Have another drink first?

—No, I've still got this one.

Looking away from the photographer, he leaned over the victrola.

—Well, I've got the bottle here, so say so when you want one.

The music started slowly, sentimentally, but he was not aware of it so much as of the silver gleam of the needle-holder meeting the silver gleam in his mind. For a moment the room seemed to revolve about the record which remained motionless. Then, with sudden impatience, he looked up. The room was motionless. The photographer was looking over the back of the loveseat toward him where he leaned on the victrola, and he was beginning to feel that he had been tricked and misled into coming here. He was almost ready to say something or to go over to the photographer when the photographer said thickly:

—When you're older it'll certainly be a shame not to have a photograph of a handsome boy like you when you were young.

And he turned his impatience back to himself and waited. After all, what did it matter to him one way or the other what the photographer did? Anything which depended partly on anybody else did not matter to him. No matter who the other person was that person would be likely to fail him. He could turn on the photographer and beat him up just for the hell of it if he wanted to. The photographer thought he was a handsome young boy, but he might change his mind for him. He could turn on him as a stag at bay sometimes turns on one of the dogs pursuing him and rips his body open with the blade of his antler. But that would not make any difference in the long run. It would only be between the photographer and him.

And as the record ended and automatically began again the idea of his omnipotence suddenly brought the inspiration which so long had eluded him.

With the gun he could do it.

A hollow of excitement and longing rose in him such as he had not felt since he had listened to Whitey in the summer night beneath the moist summer stars, invisible in the city, which splattered the country sky with their white lights, some so bright their individual beams could be seen entering the dormitory, others so faint they were only a dust of brilliance in an arc across the sky when the dogs were barking and the wind sounded like rain in the trees.

It was the first real excitement and brought with it the first real challenge he had felt since the dog days began. If he could do it, then between the easy and the impossible there would really be no difference, for between life and death there was no difference but the simple doing of this one thing. And no one would be able to change its meaning for him, to see his action in a merely personal way which confused and tricked him and opened his mind to doubt. Everybody would see that he was irrevocably right and would be sorry that they ever had denied him.

The very idea narrowed his eyes to a pinpoint of anticipatory intensity, and he saw nothing else. This was perfect. But if he did not do it, now that what it would mean had occurred to him, then he would be worse than weak. He would despise himself.

It was time for something to happen.

—Say, what do you do around here for fun?

He was looking toward the windows. The light in the street beyond had turned green, as though the last life from the trees had seeped out into the air, and the sky had turned black so that for a moment the landscape was suspended and lighter than the dark sky above. Any time now the rain would crash down and bring the cool night.

—Hey, hear what I asked?

He could not see the photographer on the loveseat so he crossed and looked down. Humped between the cushions and the back the photographer lay, his head fallen forward on his chest and both his arms twisted off the couch toward

212

the floor where his glass, stone dry, lay turned over on the rug. With a snort of disgust Blackie reached down and shook him. Dog drunk, the photographer wobbled idiotically and without resistance.

He hit the photographer's jaw hard with the knuckles of his fist. There was a crack like a twig breaking. He laughed. The disgust which he had felt passed quickly as his thoughts left the photographer and returned to himself. This proved that if what he was to do was to be important it would have to be done alone.

Turning away from the photographer he went to the retouching booth in the corner and opened the drawer. Proudly his hand reached into the back of the drawer, drew out the small cold pistol and dropped it into his pocket.

He did not give the photographer a glance. With a final disdain and determination he turned and walked out of the room, the determination and disdain in him turning to joy. He was ravished out of himself. He was converted into the prey which he pursued. He had contracted divinity into himself, as love converts into the thing loved, and though alone he was compelled within himself to hurry.

Passing by the long windows and through the arch to the vestibule, he opened the frosted glass doors and stepped out· onto the stoop. There he paused a minute, reflexively, without thought and at the bidding of the nerves buried deep within the padding of his flesh. Before him lay the city waiting for rain: the empty sky which they said was always full of planets, with no moon now, nor flowers of heaven, nor

small stars of the sod; the buildings of brick and stone, of
light and dark, unpeopled in a suspended brightness momentarily more celestial than the sky above; and across the street
the oak tree, grown great and doomed, only the sky above
it, only its own shadow on the earth below. But his gaze went
through sky and tree and shadow. He saw only himself,
companionless as the last cloud of an expiring storm whose
thunder is its knell; and descending the steps to the sidewalk he walked to the curb and straight across the street, his
movements stiff and stark, his arms held out from his sides.

The day grew dark with brilliance like a night bright with
moon and stars. Birds swerved before buildings before rain.
The sky turned black overhead and silver in a line along the
horizon, making the color yellow wherever it appeared in the
landscape, on a cereal box lying by an ashcan or on a taxi
passing the entrance of the alley, glow as though fluorescent.
The wind bowed down the trees, turning up the silver un-
dersides of their leaves, filled the air with the odor of ozone,
and from far away brought the slow rumbles of thunder, the
slow flashes of lightning and the damp comfort of rain.

The first large drops fell faster and faster, plopping
loudly on the tarpaper roofs, on the dry leaves of the trees
and on the wood of the windowsill until, falling steadily, the
rain overflowed the rainpipe at the side of the back porch
and flowed across the earth of the yard into the alley, drown-
ing the sound of its plops in a steady drone, making its own
gullies, inundating the landscape in silver.

Caleb watched from the window of his room in the house where he lived with the two old ladies, his arms folded on the windowsill and his chin resting on his arms. He liked for it to turn so dark in the daytime that lights were switched on. He liked it especially when he was in school where, while the room was brightly lighted inside, the rain in the dark outside beat down the blossoms and stalks of irises into the gravel of the yard. He liked it because the rain made him more intently aware of both himself and the world about him. And the rain comforted him as he waited and remembered that the time for his appointment with Blackie was past and that Blackie had not arrived.

Twice already the old woman whom he called Grandma had come to the door and called him to Sunday night supper. Each time he had replied that he would be there in a minute and had lain back across the bed, the sheet moist and cool against one cheek, the wind from the window cool and moist against the other, and meant to go. But each time when he sat up he remained at the window staring out at the rain, feeling his loose front tooth with his tongue and thinking that if he waited a little longer Blackie might arrive and the two of them sit down to supper together.

The sound of the rain was uninterrupted, heavy as a fountain, dark as a wood, bursting into the white foam of a waterfall out of the broken rainpipe at the side of the back porch beneath his window and flowing across the backyard and past the oak tree into the alley. He waited at the window while the sky grew light with the fall of rain and then grew dark again with dusk. And as he listened to the rain fall in the dark he was sad with the realization that Blackie was not coming. Though he could not have forgotten an appointment with Blackie, he realized that Blackie had forgotten. They were different people with different ways.

A tap came upon the door and Grandma called to him a third time.

—Honey, your supper's on the kitchen table. Come and eat now.

This time he went. The two women did not eat on Sunday night, and sitting at the table in the kitchen alone he stuffed the cold fried chicken and milk and biscuits into his mouth. As the mouthfuls of food comforted his stomach his mind was comforted also, as though only the welfare of his body mattered, and he told himself that if it had not been raining he would have gone out somewhere and have forgotten Blackie as Blackie had forgotten him. But beneath the sound of his chewing and the sound of the rain he continued to listen for footsteps coming across the porch and into the hall. He ate more slowly as the food on the plate decreased. And he looked at the slice of devil's food cake for a long time before he ate it, hoping still that Blackie would arrive and the two of them would have a hunk of cake and a cup of coffee together.

The rain fell heavily and its heavy odor in his room was as continual as its sound. When he came in from finishing his supper, comforted by the food in his stomach, he took a knife and whetting stone from the dresser and lay across the bed

216

whetting the knife back and forth on the stone in the way Blackie had shown him, listening to the high splatter of the rain on the windowsill and the low drone of the rain in the alley and the wet yard. Lonely as he never could have been in the sun, he remembered many things about his brother, how he had treated him the day he asked for the candy top, how he had walked him home many times at night and told him goodnight with affection, until Blackie assumed the variated dimensions of a person like himself, and he still hoped against hope that the rain had delayed Blackie and that he would arrive.

Then the phone rang. He stood up as he listened to the old woman shuffle along the hall to answer, and crossed to the door sure that the call would be for him. When he heard her put down the receiver on the table and shuffle toward his room he opened the door to meet her.

—It's for you, Honey.

The old woman shuffled to the end of the hall and closed the back door so he could hear over the thunder of the rain drumming on the tin back porch roof. Muffled by the closed door the rain drummed steadier and sadder as the old woman shuffled back up the hall and he lifted the receiver.

—Hello, he said into the mouthpiece.

—Hello, a muffled voice replied. Is this Caleb Pride?

He was sure that it was Blackie playing a joke on him. All of a sudden it occurred to him that perhaps they were supposed to have met somewhere else and Blackie had been waiting for him all this time just as he had been waiting for

Blackie. He was sure that it was Blackie disguising his voice and playing a joke on him, getting even by pretending that he was someone else.

—Come on, Blackie. I know it's you.

—No, this isn't Blackie. I'm calling Blackie's little brother with a message about him. His mother says for him to come over to his sister Pearl's duplex right away. Something has happened to Blackie.

—Come on, Blackie, you can't fool me.

But the voice on the phone did not seem to understand and did not drop its impersonal tone.

—Aw, come on, Blackie.

He was cut off. The receiver clicked and the line droned until the operator's nasal voice cut in asking:

—Number, please?

The rain swept in rivers along the gutters. Crossing the street Caleb stepped into water over his shoes, and the water squashed and squeaked in his shoes as he ran up the sidewalk on the other side of the street toward Ponce de Leon. He did not believe that anything had happened to Blackie. But all of a sudden it had occurred to him that it was possible, that it might have been someone else on the phone. He had run out of the house without thinking to get his raincoat, and now the rain was wetting his shirt and trickling down from his hair onto his face. At the top of the hill he stopped beneath a tree. A trolley car was streaking toward him along Ponce de Leon spraying fans of water from the tracks and spouting water from the gutters atop the roof. Out of breath he ran into the street and stood halfway between the side-walk and the trolley tracks trying not to get soaked but waving frantically to the motorman to stop.

Water streaking down the outside of the sweated windows turned the lighted signs against the black sky and the reflections of signs against the black wet pavement into writhing ribbons of color. He sat on the yellow straw seat shaking the water out of his hair onto the corrugated floor and repeating over and over to himself that nothing could have happened. If anything had happened the people on the streetcar would not be laughing and kidding. They would not be betting each other that they had already passed their theater and trying to make out through the writhing windows and the downpour where they were. He pressed his face close to the glass as they were doing and suddenly saw the big neon sign of a used car dealer. He was almost to his stop. Pushing the bell he stood up and ran through the car to the back platform. The car stopped while he was still running and threw him against the rear wall. But he regained his balance, jumped down onto the folding step before it was fully open, and bounced into the street.

The rain drenched him as he ran down the hill of Baker Street through a treeless block of garages and freight depots. He did not stop until he was at the bottom of the hill but when he reached the corner a crowd of people were standing about in the rain and he pushed his way into the crowd to see what had happened. If it were something interesting he would want to tell Blackie about it when he joined

Blackie at Pearl's place. As he pushed his way slowly through the men and women there were more of them than he had realized and he came nearer and nearer to his destination without finding out what had happened. Then he stopped behind a woman with an umbrella and a man with an unlighted cigar in his mouth. As he waited to get past he heard the woman ask what had happened and heard the man reply, the cigar moving up and down in the rain:

—Some damned fool just shot himself through the head.

Rain. Another day of rain. The sky was so limp it misted all the time it was not raining. Rain fell all morning on the trees and earth of the back yard as he watched from the window and in the afternoon, when it was time for him to go to the funeral and he left the house but walked in the opposite direction of the funeral home, fell on the deserted streets and on the black trunks and brown leaves of trees which increased as the houses became farther apart and he neared the country. With the rhythm of water and blood, of things which have happened countless times before and will happen countless times again, it fell on the wooden bridge as he passed over the railroad tracks at Howell Mill Road into the country. It fell on the group of Negro children playing in the gully of red mud before the stoop of their shack as he passed. The children looked up at him and he walked faster until he was out of their sight, then walked slowly again. He intended to run away, never to return to the city, but the strangeness of the country frightened him. He was lonely and he wanted comfort even if he had to return to the city where people did not understand. Then suddenly he stopped. He was between a lake and a dark wood. In the wood he thought he saw dead bodies hanging from the thorny branches of the trees. A street lamp flashed on above him and a group of muddy workmen were coming across the bank from the waterworks at the side of the road. The rain had stopped and against the rainwashed sky the men looked like executioners. They passed close beside him, looking at him curiously and frighteningly, and when they were past he was afraid to continue along the road behind them. Instead, he turned and looked back. The town was darker than the sky above, which was rainwashed and clear and cool. But the yellow windows of the houses were squares of warmth and comfort. Their comfort and warmth called to him, and he was too frightened to care that they lighted the houses of people whose grief was less than his own. Frightened, he walked along the black wet road toward the city, beneath departing storms and yellow skies.

AFTERWORD

From Italy, in the fall of 1948, almost a decade after I had left Atlanta for New York, I wrote to Sandy Campbell, with whom I lived, "I think this trip to Italy has done as much to make me objective and understand the things I am emotional about as my trip from Atlanta to New York did. I think the Blackie story, even the last half now, is probably close to the truth, to the way things really were or would have been."

The Dog Star and Italy do not, on first glance, seem to have much to do with each other. But it was during the summer of 1948 in Italy, from early June through the end of August, working long hours every day, in hotels in Venice, Sirmioine and Florence, that I brought the manuscript of *The Dog Star* to its final form.

The novel had been begun in the summer of 1942. I was just past my twenty-second birthday, on which I had been rejected by the draft; I was penniless, living alone in an apartment in Greenwich Village lent to me by a friend. That I would be at all able at that point to write a novel was as uncertain to me as how I was to live the rest of my life.

Three years earlier, when I had come to New York, the idea of *The Dog Star* had not yet crossed my mind. But I already knew Fred Melton, to whom the book is dedicated. It was with him, and because of him, that I had been able to leave the world I knew, the future I foresaw for myself in Atlanta, and to be responsible for my life and the things I was emotional about. To live the way I wanted to, and to write, were hardly separate in my mind; but, if one was more important than the other, it was the former.

In 1942, with Melton in the Coast Guard, married and expecting the first of his two sons, I set out on my own to begin the novel I thought of as springing from him. I had a theme. But I had no plot. No story to contain the ideas that filled my mind. No protagonist beyond a vague figure from the memories Melton had told me of his admiration for his dead brother. My only capital was my emotions; a stubborn desire to preserve them in images; and an ambition to put words together in such a manner that they *made* something rather than *said* something.

The "truth" I arrived at six years later is an "imagined" truth, the by-product of how I had lived my life throughout those years. During them, I had become convinced that, in fiction, connotation is stronger, and wears better, than denotation; my ideal was that the theme of a novel should never be stated in so many words, only by the novel as a whole; and the desired end of my objectivity was a narrative prose that would make my theme, of which I never lost sight, disappear into the story, "the way things really were or would have been."

For nearly a year after I consigned the finished novel to the agent who had handled *You Touched Me,* the play Tennessee Williams and I had written together, and which had been produced on Broadway several years earlier, she submitted it to the high-powered editors she was used to dealing with. Their reactions bewildered me. One suggested that his firm would be interested if I would change the characters to blacks. Another, that the story read like a "case history," without an author's viewpoint. None made the objection I anticipated: that I had too obviously threaded into the text phrases and echos of my theme from the writings of authors who in the past had treated the same argument, Ovid, Dante, Giordano Bruno, Shakespeare, Frazer of *The Golden Bough,* etc. Finally, I took back the novel to handle on my own. The first publishers I submitted it to accepted it. But their reason for acceptance was as odd to me as the earlier reasons for rejection: Doubleday published *The Dog Star* because it fitted into the selling category of "juvenile delinquency."

One of my goals, of course, had been to portray Atlanta, and Doubleday decided to concentrate its promotion there. The reaction of the city that had loved *Gone With the Wind* did not increase Doubleday's enthusiasm. Most of the copies with tipped-in autograph pages that were sent to Atlanta eventually turned up in New York bookstores; and the next few times I visited the city, there was no copy in the Atlanta Carnegie Public Library.

The reaction was different elsewhere. Several paperback reprints appeared in the U.S., where Thomas Mann praised it. In France, André Gide and Albert Camus arranged the book's translation and publication by Gallimard. In England, it was accepted by Rupert Hart-Davis, who continued to publish my books through the years, often before they appeared in the States.

Now, nearly fifty years later, the urban pattern of Atlanta has changed. But a great deal of the past remains, if not wholly the same. Piedmont Park remains. The summer's flower of heat still opens wide. The night skies of the dog days glitter with the same brilliance. And Blackie's problem of accepting his identity, of hunting for and fleeing from it, is still the problem of youth, perhaps more prominent. I am glad to have *The Dog Star* back in print. I hope that readers, especially southern ones, will be, too.

Donald Windham

New York, July 1998